London
May 1988

On the moors above Lessford in the dark hours just
dawn the body of a young woman is discovered. At fir
it seems that she has been thrown from a horse, but th
protruding from her ribs instantly dispels all thought
accident.

A full-scale murder investigation swings into ope
directed by Chief Superintendent Flensing, head of
Having set the wheels of the enquiry in motion – foi
tests, identification, scene of the crime details – he retui
police headquarters. As he drives through Lessfo
helicopter crashes into the city centre and all thought o
killer of the horsewoman vanishes as he and every avail
policeman, fire fighter and ambulanceman deal with
tragedy.

Alone on the moor the handful of policemen left at
scene of the murder await the promised back-up. As the
lengthens and no one arrives they take matters into their c
hands with some surprising and bizarre results.

In Lessford, the blaze under control, the dead bei
counted and the injured being attended to, the cause of t
crash is under examination – and the result of that is al
unexpected.

Once more John Wainwright displays his astonishing ran
of talents as a storyteller in this complex and chilling tale
murder.

John Wainwright
THE FORGOTTEN MURDERS

MACMILLAN
LONDON

First published in the UK 1987 by
MACMILLAN LONDON LIMITED
4 Little Essex Street London WC2R 3LF
and Basingstoke

Associated companies in Auckland, Delhi, Dublin, Gaborone, Hamburg, Harare, Hong Kong, Johannesburg, Kuala Lumpur, Lagos, Manzini, Melbourne, Mexico City, Nairobi, New York, Singapore and Tokyo

British Library Cataloguing in Publication Data

Wainwright, John, *1921-*
  The forgotten murders.
  I. Title
  832'.914[F]   PR6073.A354

  ISBN 0-333-44693-3

Typeset in Times by Bookworm Typesetting, Manchester

Printed and bound in the UK by Anchor Brendon Ltd, Essex

Police Constable Parker rubbed the stubble around his throat and, not for the first time, wished to hell he hadn't decided to go modern and grow a beard. The bewhiskered sea-dog shown on the front of an old-fashioned Players packet looked very fetching and given a few years he, Parker, might sport a similar crop but, after a mere ten days, all *he* looked was scruffy and all *he* felt was decidedly itchy.

To say nothing of the sardonic remarks uttered by Section Sergeant Reeve.

'You seem to have stood a bit too far away from the razor this morning, Parker.' Or, 'I've heard about five o'clock shadow, but this is bloody ridiculous.'

Even the super had been a mite miffed.

'Keep it trimmed, Parker. Don't just let the damn thing *grow*.'

No matter, other than the continual desire to scratch, Parker didn't worry. He wasn't the worrying kind. The Tops was a good beat and Beechwood Brook was a good division. Canteen scuttle-butt hinted at it once being a *great* division; the prowling area of a divisional officer called Ripley and even some of the hill farmers who scraped a living along The Tops told tales calculated to make a mere flatfoot's hair curl and always this guy Ripley was the one who sank battleships with his bare hands.

Parker always had the salt-cellar handy whenever he heard such stories. Bobbying was what you made it, see? In the first place it depended upon where you decided to *do* your bobbying. Play it tough and try for some inner city law-enforcement and, from time to time, you could expect anything up to and including petrol bombs. Down in The Smoke you were up to the eyeballs in Hooray Henries and Etonian twits; dumb sods who figured they hadn't had a night out until they'd spent more money than the average bloke earns in a year. Bobbying was definitely what you made it and bobbying out here on The Tops was all Parker asked for.

Heather and bracken. Mile after mile of the stuff in all directions. A criss-cross of dry-stone walls with here and there an outcrop of limestone grit and every few miles some isolated farmstead. Soothing rather than beautiful. And quiet. Peaceful. Like now – two o'clock in the morning – and a few wispy clouds playing tag with a moon that was almost full. Out there somewhere – beyond the rolled-down window of the VW – the bark of a prowling dog fox and the occasional hoot of a barn owl. Other than that only the whisper of a night breeze stroking the short-cropped vegetation.

Parker glanced at the luminous dial of his watch. Five more minutes and he'd be away. Five more minutes and Reeve could take a personal power-dive.

This was better than walkie-talkies; 'personal radio communication' was an invention geared to a high concentration of coppers all within easy distance of one nick, and out here it was all of fifteen miles to Saddlemouth police station. One day (maybe, and if he was unlucky) they'd give him a clapped-out squad car complete with transmitting and receiving gear strong enough to reach Beechwood Brook DHQ, but until then he was expected to use his own car and claim a monthly petrol allowance. Not that the petrol allowance covered the mileage – not by a long chalk – but, like most things in life, it was a swings-and-roundabouts affair. The beat boasted only one telephone kiosk, therefore if anybody (meaning Reeve) wanted to contact him it had to be at one of the previously arranged stopping points and meant a nifty little drive to the back of beyond and back. And *that* was well worth the few quid he lost on the petrol allowance swindle.

All in all it was a very nice . . .

Parker's cogitations were interrupted by the sound of galloping hoofbeats. They were coming nearer and they were going at a hell of a lick.

'What the bloody hell!'

Parker grabbed the torch from the seat alongside him, opened the car door and swung himself out of the VW and on to the road. The horse was approaching fast. At first it was a dark smudge seen in the faint gleam from the moon and against the black background of the moors and the night sky. It was going like a Derby winner with reins and stirrups flying in all directions.

Parker switched on the torch and the beam hit the horse's eyes at a range of less than ten yards. The horse reared, whinnied, pawed the air with its forelegs, dropped the forelegs back on to the surface of the road, quarter-turned, lashed out with its hind hoofs then streaked across the ling and bracken until the beam of the torch lost it in the distance.

Parker switched off the torch, leaned against the car and repeated, 'What the bloody hell!'

Parker was still leaning against the VW when Reeve arrived.

Nor was Reeve immediately convinced.

'A riderless horse?' he growled with distinct suspicion in his tone.

'Going like a bat out of hell,' insisted Parker.

'Black, was it?'

'Eh?'

'Black. These riderless horses people claim to see. They're usually black. Never piebald. Never skewbald. Always black. Black with red eyes. Yours, eh?'

'Don't you *believe* me?' Parker sounded hurt.

'Why *shouldn't* I believe you?' Reeve shook his head in mock solemnity. 'Y'know – two o'clock in the morning – miles from anywhere . . . you can't move for black, riderless horses with red eyes. You can't *move* for the bloody things.'

'Sergeant, I swear . . .'

7

'Who around here owns a black horse?'

'I didn't say it was black.'

'What colour?'

'Dark,' ventured Parker. 'It was dark coloured.'

'Black.'

'Sergeant, I don't know. I can't be *sure*.'

'Now that,' said Reeve, 'is what I call bloody good observation. A man sees a horse – a copper who's been trained at great expense to use his eyes – he sees a horse. Not a cat. Not a dog. A damn great horse, as big as a house side – and he can't remember what colour it was.'

'Sarge, I'm sorry, but . . . '

'You're sure it *was* a horse? Not a camel? Not an elephant?'

'Sergeant, it was a sodding great *horse*.' Parker was losing his patience. This self-opinionated section sergeant of his was deliberately needling him and Parker didn't like it. There was a touch of impatience in his voice as he continued, 'It was coming *at* me, like Joe Fury. I don't particularly like horses. I don't *understand* the damn things. I flashed my torch in its face and that seemed to scare it. It wasn't as scared as *I* was – I thought the frigging thing was going to trample me underfoot – but it was scared enough to take off over the heather.' Parker raised an arm and pointed. 'That's where it went. Christ only knows where it *came* from.'

'Lock that car of yours.' Reeve sounded almost convinced. 'We'll take my jalopy and snoop round a bit.'

2

'Reeve, d'you know what time it is?' Hobart asked the question and answered it in his next sentence. 'Twenty minutes past three. Ante meridiem, sergeant. Not in the afternoon. A time when all good men – even police sergeants and detective inspectors – should be fast asleep in bed. Not tooling around in the UK equivalent of Outer Mongolia finding bodies.'

Hobart wished it was like they showed things on the movies or on TV. Bedside telephones and a man young enough and fit enough to leap from between the sheets, buckle on a pair of jeans and hare off in a supercharged sports car. But it wasn't *like* that. Not in real life. By the time you reached detective inspector you were just about ready for the knacker's yard. All the juice had been squeezed out of you.

He grumbled into the mouthpiece of the phone, 'All right, sergeant. I *know* you can't sit on it till morning. Just don't make *me* something special. Get 'em all out. The super, Hoyle, Flensing . . . everybody. When I get out there I don't even want the birds to be asleep.'

From the bedroom a woman's voice called, 'Clarence! Are you downstairs, Clarence?'

Hobart ignored the question and spoke into the mouthpiece again.

'Get hold of a squad car. Fix *some* sort of radio link with civilisation. Then get back there and wait. For God's sake don't leave Parker alone for too long. And – from me – any size eleven footprints trampling clues into the mud and I'll have somebody's tripes on a plate.'

'Clarence! Is that you, Clarence?'

Hobart dropped the receiver on to its rest and, as he slowly climbed the stairs, he said, 'Yes, Fiona, it's me. It had *better* be me, otherwise we've been burgled.'

'We've been *what*?' She sat bolt upright in the king-sized bed as he entered the room.

'Nothing, dear.'

'You said we'd been . . .'

'I was being funny, dear,' sighed Hobart. 'I was trying to cheer myself up.'

'Can't you sleep?' she demanded, and the words had a ring of accusation. 'I *told* you. That blue stilton you had for supper. You were so sure it wouldn't . . .'

'The telephone. Not cheese.' Hobart tossed his pyjama jacket and trousers on to the bed and looked ridiculous clad only in a string vest. He had a sudden urge to empty his bladder and, as he made for the bathroom, said, 'Fiona, it wasn't the best idea of your life to have that hall tiled. It's like standing on ice.'

'You have slippers. You should have . . .'

'I didn't.' He spoke from the bathroom. 'I keep forgetting we now have a hall with a temperature on a par with Antarctica. Answering the telephone in this house isn't far short of taking a crash course of commando training.'

'Oh! Was it the telephone?'

'Yes, dear.'

'I thought it must be the cheese.'

'Not the cheese, dear.' He flushed the toilet and padded back into the bedroom. 'Cheese doesn't make me do these things.'

'What things?'

'Strip off, before I go for a pee.'

'Was it Morgan?' she asked, with sudden interest.

'Fiona, why on earth should our dearly beloved son telephone us at this hour?' He struggled into underpants, then sat on a chair and reached for his socks. 'Morgan,' he added, glumly, 'will be tucked up in bed with his latest conquest.'

'Youth will have its fling.' She smiled. 'They're very broad-minded at universities, you know.'

'I know.' He panted a little as he struggled with the socks. A pot-belly didn't make for easy bending. He added, 'I know . . . but I don't fully approve. I am, as you know, paying through the nose for our offspring to end up with a degree. Not, necessarily, a degree in fornication.'

'He's *young*.'

'I suppose,' sighed Hobart, 'that *I* was young – once. I'm damned if I remember it.'

'You were quite a catch,' she assured him.

'You loved me?' He reached for his shirt.

'Of course.'

'You *still* love me?'

'Naturally.'

'Good.' He threaded his arms through the sleeves. 'Nip down to the kitchen and make me some strong, black coffee.'

'I thought you couldn't sleep. That won't . . .'

'Not *couldn't* sleep, dear. Not *allowed* to sleep. There's a body up on The Tops. "Suspicious circumstances", as the saying goes. This job of mine – the job which pays for you putting floor tiles in the hall – the job that enables our son, Morgan, to make himself favourite in the Casanova Stakes – requires that I go there and make a complete fool of myself.'

3

Parker was not as happy as he'd been an hour or so previously. Outside the shelter of a motor car it was very nippy. That night breeze he'd noticed with some personal approval wasn't at all welcome standing there without even the added warmth of a mac. Even the moon seemed to have developed a distinctly icy stare.

But, at least, Reeve now believed him. There hadn't been much choice once the headlights of Reeve's car had picked out the figure sprawled in the middle of the road. Jodhpurs, riding-boots, waistcoat and a hunting-pink jacket equated with a nag, and the riding-helmet which had rolled a couple of yards from the dead woman intimated that she hadn't been out for a midnight stroll.

The knife wasn't nice. Very nasty, in fact. Very off-putting. In between the ribs and, if the hilt was anything to go by, driven hard and at a deliberate angle.

Parker flapped his arms and stamped his feet to get the circulation going a bit faster. Then he crouched on his

11

haunches, shone the beam of his torch into the dead woman's face and tilted his head in an attempt at possible recognition.

A typical horsey type by the look of things. Slightly buck-toothed. But very *good* teeth; very white and very clean. Not much make-up. Maybe a touch of lipstick and a light dusting of face-powder, but no eye-shadow. High cheek bones; what the artistic crowd called 'fine bone structure'. The chin looked a little pushy – as if she could be a bit of a bitch if the mood took her – but that was par for the course. Horsey people *did* tend to be stroppy. Maybe it had something to do with always being saddle-sore.

Parker moved the torch beam slightly and caught his breath. The sightless eyes emphasised the mistake of his thoughts. She could *have been* a bit of a bitch. But no more. No more hunt balls. No more stirrup-cups. No more rolls in the horse-box hay.

But, no – he didn't know her. It was a hell of a beat and he didn't lay claim to knowing everybody who lived in the umpteen isolated dwellings. But he knew most of them and he was pretty sure he'd have known this one. *She* would have made sure of that. She was that sort. He'd met too many not to recognise outward appearances. On top of which, blushing violets didn't tog themselves up in fancy gear and take midnight rides along The Tops.

He switched off the torch and straightened to a standing position.

Beyond a distant rise tilted headlights wiped the horizon and the flick of hinted fluorescent blue showed the approach of a squad car complete with flashing roof-light.

4

It was only a narrow road – no wider than to allow two cars to pass with moderate safety – therefore the canvas screens which now surrounded the body effectively blocked the passage of vehicles other than via the close-cropped grass which flanked the tarmacadam. The earth beneath the grass was spongy and already one lunatic driving a bread van had ripped the turf away from the underlying peat and had had to be manhandled back on to the hard surface.

It was about an hour past dawn, a local medic had been roused from his bed to officially pronounce 'life extinct' and now they were waiting for the people with various qualifications to examine the body prior to Flensing slamming things into overdrive and getting a full-scale murder enquiry under way. As always, in this sort of situation, men stood around in groups. They talked, and their talk covered a multitude of subjects. It rarely touched upon murder.

'A class batsman,' Hoyle was insisting, 'should never be caught other than behind the wicket. Okay, you get a good bowler who can swing the ball. A fast or fast-medium. Even a good spinner. He can make the best batsman in the world edge one into the slips or into the wicket-keeper's gloves. But when a batsman commits himself to a clean, forward stroke he should *know*. At grass-level or over their heads.'

'A typical Yorkshire generality,' grunted Reeve. 'Dammit, the West Indian speed merchants deliberately short-pitch 'em. Get a cricket ball coming at your head at damn near a hundred miles an hour . . . you have to do *something*.'

'Duck,' suggested Hoyle. 'Let them bowl themselves to death. It's been done in the past. Sutcliffe could do it.'

'It's a different game, these days,' contributed Flensing.

'Oh, no.' Hoyle shook his head. 'It's just *played* different-ly. The crash-bang-wallop crowd have taken over. There isn't the finesse there used to be.'

Cricket. The great leveller. A detective chief superintendent, a detective chief inspector and a section sergeant, but rank was ignored and each claimed expertise enough to argue the other two off the face of the earth. Nor were they wasting time. When nothing *could* be done nothing *should* be done. The trick was to *know* something – to fill a vacuum with as many facts as possible – thereafter to add to that knowledge as fast as possible. Graft by the bucketful was

13

going to be available within the next few hours. Meanwhile – and no disrespect to the corpse – stay relaxed and talk cricket.

Hobart was saying, 'So what the deuce do they mean when they describe it as a "Friday" car? Would they object if I paid for it with a "Friday" cheque?'

'Some cars are rogue cars,' explained the Road Traffic Section sergeant. 'I've known some cars . . . the best drivers in the world couldn't have kept them from accidents.'

'That's not what I'm getting at. It's just that . . . '

'It's an expression,' offered Parker. 'The last car of the week. Everybody's tired. Everybody's looking forward to the weekend. They tend to be a bit slipshod.'

'There's nothing "slipshod" about the price. Every time you buy one the infernal thing costs a few hundred pounds more than it did last time.'

'I've known cars . . . ' The Road Traffic Section sergeant was going to say his piece whether or not it was relevant. 'I've known *drivers* – level-headed, sensible men – but, could you get them behind the wheel of a car that had been in an accident – especially a fatal accident? No way! They wouldn't *sit* in the thing. It had blood on its bodywork, see? It was a killer.'

They talked about motor cars. They even touched upon the subject of fatal road accidents. But the conversation was in no way related to the dead woman behind the canvas screens. She was something else. A different subject. A subject which, in time, would occupy their minds to the exclusion of all else.

But, for the moment, cricket – motor cars . . . anything.

The caller said, 'I wish to report the fact that my daughter didn't come home last night.'

'Who's calling, please?' The policewoman constable on switchboard duty at Beechwood Brook DHQ eased a pad of flimsies nearer and picked up a ballpoint.

'Andrew Cossitter.'

Thereafter followed the required questions and answers concerning address and telephone number.

'What's your daughter's name, please?' asked the policewoman constable.

'Anthea. Anthea Cossitter.'

'And when did she leave home?'

'Yesterday afternoon. Immediately after lunch. At about two o'clock.'

'Did she say where she was going?'

'To visit a friend. An old schoolfriend. Mary Perkins. She lives at Apple Tree Farm. Just this side of Haggthorpe. I've telephoned. They say she left for home early yesterday evening. At about eight o'clock . . .'

6

Within the confines of the canvas screens the subject was murder. Not motor cars – not cricket – *murder*. Flensing, Hoyle and Hobart stood with their backs to the canvas and watched. All three concentrated because all three knew that at some time in the future some defending barrister would pounce upon any mistake – any discrepancy in their respective evidence – and magnify that mistake until it sounded at best like stupidity and at worst like deliberate perjury.

'She's married.' Flensing moved his head in a tiny nod at the gold band. 'Some husband, somewhere, could be missing her.'

The pathologist unbuttoned the waistcoat and the shirt and placed the flat of his hand on the stomach.

The three detectives stood motionless, with their hands deep in the pockets of their coats. More basic procedure. See everything, but touch *nothing*. Hopefully, only two men had touched the corpse. The medic who'd verified death and now the pathologist. Any other signs of handling could point the enquiry into a specific direction. As with the hands, so with the feet. Reeve and Parker had been questioned. Parker hadn't been within two yards of the body. Reeve had been close enough to squat down and touch the artery in the neck to check she wasn't still alive. Assuming they weren't lying – assuming neither of them wanted to cover up a silly mistake – the area immediately around the corpse might – just *might* – give some slender lead.

It was known as the Theory of Transference and it sounded great when explained. On paper it was foolproof. It was impossible – quite impossible – for two surfaces to touch without some tiny and perhaps invisible part of Surface A being transferred to Surface B – and vice versa, of course. Home Office Detective Courses tended to go mildly gaga about the Theory of Transference. Forensic scientists swore by it. And, okay, it worked – sometimes. Dust, the debris resultant upon a car accident, seeds, hairs. These things *had* stood men in a dock in the past. Just don't put *all* your money on that little number.

Nevertheless, and because they needed *something* with which to trigger off the initial man-hunt, Flensing, Hoyle and Hobart kept their feet still in case they knocked the Theory of Transference for a loop.

The pathologist was wrenching at the fingers, trying to straighten them. He was a prematurely bald man, in his early fifties, and those hands of his could both grip and lever. They

16

were the tools of his somewhat grisly trade. Like the hands of a surgeon – or the hands of a highly skilled carpenter – they represented controlled power.

From beyond the canvas a voice said, 'Chief Superintendent Flensing, sir.' It was a loud whisper, as if the speaker didn't want to interrupt anything.

Flensing turned his head to look through the opening in the canvas screen.

The Motor Patrol Section sergeant stretched out a hand holding a folded piece of paper.

'Over the radio, sir. A Missing from Home. It sounds as if it might be her.'

'Thank you, sergeant.'

Flensing removed a hand from its pocket, reached out, took the billet and, without reading it, returned the hand to its pocket. There was a deliberation in everything. A cold lack of excitement. The pathologist who was now easing the lids clear of the dead eyes. The terse 'Thank you, sergeant.' The expressionless faces of the three officers. Even the ever-present breeze seemed to change its pattern; instead of gusting it blew steadily and kept the canvas of the screens in a silent strain against the posts.

The pathologist re-buttoned the shirt and waistcoat, touched the cravat into its original position, then eased the corpse back to how it had sprawled prior to his examination.

As he straightened to an upright position, he said, 'That's it, gentlemen. I'll let you know more when I've had her in the mortuary.'

He left the shelter of the canvas surround and the three detectives followed. They distanced themselves in a group from the other officers before anybody spoke.

'Well?' asked Flensing.

'Time of death – a very rough estimate.' The pathologist nipped his bottom lip with his teeth for a moment. 'No later than eight o'clock last night. At a guess, some time before. The temperature out here, at night, plays ducks and drakes

17

with things. I suggest you play things safe. Assume, with some certainty, that she was dead at eight o'clock.'

'Eight o'clock?' murmured Hobart.

Hoyle said, 'That means she was *brought* here,' and voiced the obvious.

The pathologist stooped to dust the knees of his trousers, then straightened, gave a quick and fleeting smile and said, 'It's all yours now, chief superintendent. The result of the PM should be on your desk by this evening.'

He left the group and walked towards his waiting car. Flensing twisted his expression into a moue of concentration before he spoke. First he turned to Hoyle.

'David, you're the field commander. Stay here until things are more or less back to normal. The usual pattern. Photographs. Sketch plans. An on-the-knees search. Do you think the dogs?'

'Not the dogs,' replied Hoyle. 'At least, not yet. Given the chance, they'll piss and crap over everything.'

'Even the best of them,' agreed Flensing with a smile. 'If you feel you need them, yell. Get men in from the division. As many as you need. Road blocks. All drivers and passengers to be asked when they last drove along this road. If it was yesterday – at *any* time – names and addresses for follow-up enquiries.' He paused, glanced at the surrounding moorland, then asked, 'A mobile Incident Centre?'

'Wasted.' Hoyle didn't hesitate.

'I tend to agree. I'll set up an Information Room at DHQ. Meanwhile keep enough squad cars on the scene to have a permanent radio link. Oh, and keep Reeve and Parker handy for any local knowledge they may have.' Another pause, then, 'Anything else?'

'I can't think of anything.'

'Fine. If you *do* think of anything use your initiative and *my* rank, if necessary. I'll let Alva know where you are, and I'll be out again, later.' A tight half-smile, then, 'Meanwhile, beware Harris.'

'I'll keep things on the simmer.'

'Good.' Flensing turned to Hobart, held out the note the Motor Patrol Section sergeant had handed him, and said, 'A Missing from Home. It came in while we were behind the screens. It might be the victim. Check it out. Take a plain-clothes man with you. If it *is* the victim follow it up and keep me informed.'

7

The murderer shaved with his usual care and concentration. He sliced away the thick, creamy lather with slow deliberate strokes then finger-tipped the baby-smooth skin with something not far removed from erotic pleasure.

He was a fastidious man and this early-morning ritual of cleansing himself was always the first highlight of his day. He was a man of habit and the pattern rarely varied and was never rushed.

His orderly and unvariable life style was known to his friends. Equally, it was known to his enemies. As head of his own wine-importing business he planed to Paris on the same scheduled flight on the first Tuesday of every month. He always stayed at the Hotel Opal in the Rue Tronchet but took most of his meals at the restaurant 'Chez Louis' in the Rue Lincoln.

He was a homosexual but did nothing to either hide or advertise his preference; merely that his Parisian evenings were spent in the select but secluded little clubs off the Rue La Boette where, instead of French whores, he picked up French faggots.

He had no permanent 'lover'. That would have been a commitment to somebody other than himself and he was far too selfish a person for that. Instead, he had a string of obliging young men of a like disposition, any of whom he could telephone to share his bed when the mood took him.

By any normal standards he was a rich man and he lived up to his income. The house stood in its own four acres of well-cared-for garden and for a man living alone, which was his normal mode of life, it was a ridiculously large house; seven bedrooms, three bathrooms, a dining room, a lounge, a study and a huge excellently equipped kitchen; these plus pantries, walk-in food stores, lumber rooms and similar bits and pieces.

He employed no live-in help, but two gardeners and three daily cleaning ladies kept the place immaculate by their unseen presence.

The inhabitants of the nearby village only knew him as 'odd' – 'funny' – 'a queer 'un' – but rusticity being what it is they would have used the same expression about any well-heeled man unwilling to join them with a tankard of ale at the local pub.

Had he been asked – had he been prepared to give an answer – the man might have claimed that he sought privacy without feeling cramped. That he was a person with expansive and expensive tastes but at the same time, and for much of his life, he was a person satisfied with his own company. Much of what the second half of the twentieth century had to offer left him unmoved; the average person of that particular era was either a bore or a lout. Nevertheless, he was happy to wallow in whatever comforts present-day ingenuity could provide.

Hence the bathroom in which he was enjoying his morning shave.

Above the vanity unit – immediately below the room-length mirror – a broad, glass shelf held an assortment of expensive talcs and lotions. At one end of the shelf a transistor radio gave the murderer an accompaniment of classical music to his ablutions.

The Chicago Symphony Orchestra played the opening bars of Bartok's *Concerto for Orchestra* as he dropped his pyjama trousers into the wickerwork 'Ali Baba' basket and stepped behind the frosted glass of the shower cubicle. It was one of the few modern pieces he rather liked.

8

Hoyle knew The Tops. He'd known them when Ripley was around; when Ripley had been the uniformed chief superintendent in charge of Beechwood Brook Division and *he'd* been a mere detective constable in Lessford City Police. Before the monumental snarl-up of 'amalgamation'. In the old days, when Lessford and Bordfield had had their own forces; when a county constabulary which included Beechwood Brook had its own subtle way of bobbying. The 'county' way. The 'Ripley' way.

He (Hoyle) had worked under Ripley on his first murder enquiry, and a first murder enquiry was like the first time you make love to a woman. Special. Always remembered. And that one had been *worth* remembering.*

And Ripley had helped. Ripley had encouraged. Ripley had given him more freedom of action than any mere detective constable had the right to expect. Ripley . . . God rest his soul.

A friend. Despite their difference in rank and that they were from different forces, a friend. A friend, and the most complete copper Hoyle had ever met. Good coppers came with a fairly frequent regularity – he could name at least half a dozen good coppers – but Ripley had been more than that. He'd been a *great* copper. He'd had that extra something – that indescribable charismatic quality – you only come across once in a lifetime. And The Tops had been part of his stamping ground. The Tops had been where they'd first met. Beechwood Brook had been Ripley's personal fiefdom.

Hoyle felt strangely guilty as he brought his wandering

* See *Portrait in Shadows* by John Wainwright, Macmillan, London, 1986.

thoughts under control. *Flensing* was his friend, these days. Flensing was his friend, his gaffer, a detective chief superintendent and head of the Lessford Region CID. It was wrong, therefore, that Flensing should be compared with a long-dead policeman, however good that policeman might have been. However *great* he might have been. The damn job had changed. The way of *doing* the job had changed. Maybe, today, Ripley wouldn't be the ball of fire he'd been in the old days. Maybe balls of fire had gone out with the yoyo and the hula-hoop. Maybe anything . . . just that comparisons couldn't be made and it was unfair to try.

'That's us finished, chief inspector.'

Hoyle blinked himself back to the present as a sergeant from the Photography Section spoke.

'Er – good. Good.' Hoyle cleared his throat. He asked, 'The Plan Drawing crowd?'

'I'd say about another half hour.'

'Good.'

The sergeant said, 'We'll take a morgue shot, for identification purposes, before the pathologist opens her up.'

'Oh – er – yes.' Hoyle made a final effort and gathered his thoughts. 'Try not to make her look *too* dead, sergeant.'

'Eh?'

'We think she may be a Missing from Home, already reported. We may need a photograph for initial identification purposes.'

'She's dead, sir,' the sergeant reminded him.

'Make it look as though she's asleep.'

'Sir . . .' The sergeant hesitated, then said, 'She'll be on the slab. Okay – just head and shoulders – but we can't make her look *alive*.'

'It's your department, sergeant.' There was a tight, hard quality to Hoyle's tone. 'I'm not asking for an Anthony Armstrong-Jones job. Just a little less harsh than usual. A little more *humane*. Make believe she's *your* daughter. That you don't yet know she's dead. That you're going to be shown *that* photograph – and that the photograph isn't going

22

to shock you too much.'

'We'll – er – we'll do our best, sir.'

'Do that,' grunted Hoyle.

9

Flensing heard the explosion before he saw the mass of flame and smoke in the sky. Flensing was a detective chief superintendent and his training, plus a lifetime of experience, had taught him how to register every happening; how to break it down into split-second component parts. He had been driving to his office at Lessford Police Headquarters, to check the build-up of paperwork prior to a return to Beechwood Brook DHQ and the murder enquiry, when one part of his mind had registered the throb of helicopter blades. Then had come a bang followed by a roar.

There'd been two distinct but linked sounds. A shell-burst crack and a thunder of noise which seemed to trail away and curve into silence. Something very much like an acoustic semicolon.

Flensing braked the car to a halt by the kerb then leaned forward and squinted upwards through the windscreen.

He saw flame – he saw wreckage falling from the sky – but the 'ball of fire' analogy had no meaning. The scarlet, yellow and orange had no shape. The thick, oily smoke etched meaningless patterns in and around the blazing, tumbling pieces.

Flensing put the car into first, then moved rapidly into third gear, the better to control the car at speed through traffic-packed streets. He flicked the headlights on to 'beam' and when he didn't need both hands on the wheel he kept the heel of one hand on the horn button. He claimed the right to overtake on the nearside when he couldn't overtake on the off. Twice he chose a short cut by snaking his way through oncoming traffic in face of a one-way-street flow.

The city centre was in turmoil. The heart of the chaos was in the area around the central library and art gallery and Flensing left the car and sprinted the last fifty yards or so.

One corner of the library-cum-art-gallery had been sliced away and flames were already spreading. Windows had smashed and shattered glass was underfoot as he ran. Cars had collided and one van had mounted the pavement and crashed its nose through the plate glass of a café window. Women were screaming and men were shouting and, for the last few yards, Flensing had to elbow his way to the scene.

Eventually order would be restored but for the moment the impression was that of a boiling cauldron overflowing with noise and dust and fire.

A handful of constables were already trying to create some sort of order and as Flensing arrived two squad cars, lights flashing and sirens howling, eased their way along the pavement to where they might do most good.

'The Fire Service?' Flensing snapped the question at the first constable he reached.

'Look, you'd better . . .' The constable recognised the detective chief superintendent and continued, 'Sorry, sir. Yes, the Fire Service *has* been sent for. And the Ambulance Service. People are inside that building. At a guess . . .'

Flensing had learned what he wanted to know. He hurried to one of the squad cars and rapped out orders.

'Radio for as many men as possible. Keep the crowds back. Shift some of those vehicles and make a passage for the fire and ambulance people. Then, do what you can to divert ordinary traffic.' As the Motor Patrol officer leaned into his vehicle and unclipped the microphone, Flensing added, 'Tell them I'm here, but that we need a uniformed superintendent and some sergeants at the scene to take over responsibility for getting something sorted out.'

The fire was spreading. As Flensing turned from the squad car a section of the library wall collapsed inwards in a shower of sparks and a sudden gout of flame.

'Where in hell's name is that Fire Service,' snarled Flensing and as if in answer to his helpless fury the first scarlet vehicle threaded its way through the tangle of traffic and men trained in speed and efficiency raced to lay the first of the lacework of hoses. Eventually a blaze which at present raged unhindered would be under control.

Flensing breathed a sigh of relief and dropped his chin on to his chest – and, for the moment, gave no thought to a murder victim out on The Tops.

10

Andrew Cossitter was one of those small, aggressive men. Had he been part of the canine world he would have been a terrier. Even his voice had a certain high-pitched yapping quality.

'What is this?' he demanded. Then, before Hobart could reply, 'I'm not a fool, you know.'

'Your daughter,' said Hobart, gently. 'You reported her as a Missing from Home.'

'What's happened?' Cossitter moved around on elbow crutches. He seemed to have difficulty swivelling the pelvic region of his body and beneath the trousers both legs were stiff and unbending. The rubber bosses on the ends of the crutches made tiny squeaking noises on the polished floor of the room. He snapped, 'Something's happened to her. Don't piss around trying to humour me. Let's have it.'

'Mr Cossitter . . .' began Hobart.

'Him, perhaps.' Cossitter raised one of the elbow crutches enough to indicate he meant the watching detective constable. 'I expected the local constable. But a detective *inspector*.'

'When did you see Anthea last?' asked Hobart, patiently.

'I've already told your people. About two o'clock yesterday afternoon.'

'She left for Apple Tree Farm?'

25

'You have it all there.' Cossitter glared at the square of paper Hobart held in his hand. 'Apple Tree Farm. One of her friends – a friend from her school-days – one of her *many* friends. They tell me she left at about eight o'clock. She hasn't got back yet.'

'Where else might she be?' asked Hobart, quietly.

'How the devil do I know.' Cossitter compressed his lips and inhaled deeply through his nose. He barked, 'Inspector, let me make things easier for you. I don't like my daughter. I don't approve of her life style. Equally, she dislikes me. All this moonshine about parental love doesn't wash in this household. Which means I'm not likely to faint – throw a fit – anything like that.'

'If . . . *what*?' smiled Hobart.

'If she's been assaulted. Raped. Dead. Anything.'

'Do you think she has?'

'Until you tell me, how the devil do I know?'

'Do you think she *might* have been?'

'You.' Cossitter spoke to the detective constable. He jerked his head in the direction of a glass-fronted wall-cabinet. 'Pour three whiskies. Make mine a stiff one.'

'Not for me,' murmured Hobart. 'It's too early in the day.'

'Make it two.' Then, as the DC hesitated, 'Good God, man. Don't just *stand* there. It's good malt whisky, but it won't pour itself.'

'Have one if you wish,' smiled Hobart.

'Thank you, sir.' Then, to Cossitter, 'Thank *you*, sir.'

As the DC poured the drinks Cossitter stumped to a deep armchair and lowered himself into its comfort. His legs stuck out in front of him in a V, with no bend at the knees.

He accepted the whisky, tasted it, then said, 'Right. I'm sitting down. I have booze at hand if the shock's too great. Go ahead. Break the news.'

'We think she's dead,' said Hobart, flatly.

'Think?'

'If it's your daughter.'

'I gave a description.'

26

'That's why we think it's her.'

'There's her photograph.' Cossitter waved a hand. 'One of those on the grand.'

Hobart walked to the grand piano, picked up one of the framed photographs standing on its surface and studied it.

'Well?' demanded Cossitter.

'I think so.' Hobart nodded. 'It's difficult to be positive – this being a wedding photograph – but . . .'

'Let's assume it *is* my daughter you're on about.'

'In that case, we should contact her husband.'

'Please do.' Cossitter tasted the whisky. 'And, when you find him, let me know. I'll break his blasted neck.'

'He left her?' suggested Hobart.

'*She* left *him*,' grunted Cossitter. 'She left *him*, then came racing back to *me* . . . and he was away and gone to hell, somewhere in South America before I could sling her back. That's why she's gone back to her maiden name. To annoy me as much as possible.'

'On the assumption we're talking about your daughter, Anthea . . .'

'That's what we're assuming.'

'I have to tell you she was murdered at some time last night. Late evening, we think.'

'Across at Apple Tree Farm?'

'We don't know that, yet,' said Hobart, quietly. 'All we know, at the moment, is that she was stabbed and that her body was found out on The Tops in the early hours of this morning.'

'It had to happen,' muttered Cossitter, savagely. 'God damn it, it *had* to happen. Some people are born to come to a sticky end. That stupid bitch was one of them.'

Hobart moistened his lips, then said, 'The offer of that drink. Does it still stand?'

'Of course.'

Hobart glanced at the detective constable and the DC moved towards the wall-cabinet.

There was nothing left to suggest that the body of a murdered woman had been there. Two squad cars and a couple of police signs instructing drivers to stop. Hoyle's car and Reeve's car. Four Motor Patrol officers, Reeve, Parker and Hoyle himself. The body had been moved. So had the canvas screens. The few vehicles which had passed that way had already disturbed the dust and now there was nothing. A very ordinary vehicular shunt-up would have left far more signs.

'Mark the spot, sergeant.' Hoyle spoke to Reeve. 'A stone – something – otherwise we'll be guessing.'

'I know this beat, sir.' Parker sounded mildly offended by Hoyle's instructions to Reeve. He pointed as he continued, 'Down there there's an Ordnance Survey point. In the other direction there's an outcrop. I've paced it from both. I know *exactly* where the body was.'

'Something,' insisted Hoyle. 'Some sort of marker. For *her* sake as much as for ours.'

Reeve left them, and Hoyle spoke to Parker.

'The curate's cat has kittens,' he murmured. 'It's your beat. You should know.'

'Yes, sir. I *would* know.'

'Who rides across the moor?'

'Nobody.'

'That's a cop out, Parker. That's . . .'

'No, sir.' Parker squinted towards the mauve-coloured haze which shimmered the far horizon. 'Out Pinthead way a few people have nags. There's even an annual point-to-point. But not in these parts. A couple of years ago one of the hill farmers hit upon the idea of using a pony to round up his sheep. He was given the hard word. No horses. No vehicles, except on permitted paths. It's shooting country, sir.'

'Oh!'

'Partridge and grouse. I'm told there's some ptarmigan – but that's something I *haven't* seen.'

'One must not disturb the game,' muttered Hoyle, sourly.

'That's the top and bottom of it, sir. A day's shooting across this land costs money.'

'These "permitted paths" you mention. Do you know them?'

'Most of them. I sometimes leave the car and wander around a bit. Some bloody fool slings an empty bottle. This time of year you could have a rare old fire in no time at all.'

'They're not *secret* paths, then?'

'No, sir.' Parker looked mildly surprised. 'Ramblers. Conservationists. Botanists, even. A couple of times I've come across campers – paraffin stove going full throttle.'

'Show me some of these paths.' Hoyle seemed to reach a decision. 'We'll leave Sergeant Reeve here, while you and I take a walk.'

12

Gilliant had been a chief constable more years than he sometimes cared to contemplate. He'd worked his way up through the ranks. He'd paused for passing acquaintanceship with the Regional Crime Squad set-up. He'd lingered for a while within the secrecy of the provincial Special Branch. Thereafter he'd remained with CID until, eventually, he'd taken over command of Lessford Metropolitan Police District; the bumper-bundle job which had swallowed the twin cities of Lessford and Bordfield plus most of the surrounding county constabulary area.

Use whichever yardstick you liked – acreage, population or authorised police strength – it was one hell of a responsibility and yet one which Gilliant carried with apparent ease.

Since he'd taken over that responsibility he'd had many and varied communications with Whitehall. Home Office circulars, for example, could be as thick as leaves in late autumn when some hothead came up with some new and screwy idea with the intention of making a name for himself.

Gilliant wasn't wildly enthusiastic about Whitehall whiz-kids.

He drummed his fingers on the telephone receiver he'd just returned to its rest. It had not been a good day; not one of the jolliest days of his life. First the woman murdered on The Tops. Then the helicopter crash. And now *this*. All this infernal hush-hush stuff. What had happened in the centre of Lessford came under the heading of 'Disaster' and short of a D Notice clamp-down the media people would sniff something out, and if they *did* . . .

Instinct – gut reaction if you like – warned Gilliant that he was being eased behind the eight ball and Gilliant had been in the job far too long to dismiss gut reactions.

He sighed before lifting the receiver from its rest and speaking to the officer on duty at the switchboard.

'Chief constable here. Put me through to the assistant chief constable (crime). Then get somebody to fix us up with a quick meal. Tea and sandwiches . . . something like that. Here in my office in about half an hour, please.'

13

Nobody knows how the media get to know about these things, nor how they get to know so *quickly*. Merely let there be an accident, a tragedy, a political scandal, a municipal uproar or even some public clown making a fool of himself and (or so it seems) inaudible jungle drums send the appropriate code words and, almost before the dust has had time to settle, characters armed with pencils and notebooks, cameras and microphones are there probing and prodding, asking and recording, photographing and pontificating.

BBC and ITV – both national and regional – were there.

Newspaper reporters and cameramen shouldered their way to some eyewitness or some vantage point. Sudden death was news. Carnage was the stuff upon which both viewers and readers must be fed. Lessford could, for the moment, elbow round-the-world minor battle fronts from top spot . . . therefore, keep pushing, friend, and refuse to *be* pushed.

The Fire Service had mastered the blaze and were concentrating on containing what heat remained within the collapsed interior of the library and art gallery. The hoses were still plentiful but some of the larger appliances had returned to their bases.

Flensing was still there, but he'd been joined by a uniformed superintendent, and a uniformed inspector. Two uniformed sergeants were in charge of the coppers and where there had once been far too few coppers there now seemed to be too many. Mobile barricades had been placed in position and pedestrians were being encouraged to, 'Move along, please.' The traffic was rolling again and although it tended to slow and bottleneck as drivers followed diversion signs there was movement where at one time there had been a phalanx of stationary vehicles.

As a city, Lessford had been wounded and at the moment of wounding it had suffered a shock. But in Hitler's war it had accepted its share of bombs and like other cities it had shaken the débris from its hair, hauled itself to its feet and grinned scarred defiance at those who had mauled it.

The chief librarian was of a generation which had lived through those years.

'A bit like old times,' he observed and although it was unintentional his tone carried the barest hint of nostalgia. 'The same smell of dust and burned out bonfires. The same muck underfoot.'

'I wouldn't know.' The art gallery curator was a much younger man. *His* philosophy was firmly entagled around an emotion he chose to call 'love' and a passion for what he was pleased to describe as 'non-violence'. In a slightly petulant voice he added, 'All this destruction sickens me. It makes me positively ill.'

'Of course.' The words were flat and unemotional. They could have been taken to mean anything. The librarian's very private opinion was that the curator was a gutless young prat with very little gumption and even less experience. He murmured, 'Some of your favourite art treasures have gone for a burton.'

'Of course.'

'I'm sorry,' said the librarian, and meant it.

'Irreplaceable.' The curator stood with his hand on his head, as if in pain, as they stared at what was left of their respective responsibilities. He repeated, 'Quite, *quite* irreplaceable.'

'Tough luck.'

'We covered such a wide spectrum.'

'I don't know much about paintings.' The librarian pushed his hands deeper into the pockets of his trousers. 'Not much about art, generally. Far too many imponderables for a simple-minded bloke like me.'

'If not destroyed, ruined beyond repair,' moaned the curator.

'Aye – a pity.'

'All that water. A ridiculous amount of water.'

'It was necessary,' explained the librarian. 'The place was burning.'

'They used too much water. *Far* too much water.'

'It was a fair old blaze. We were both lucky to get out alive.'

'I chose with such care.' The curator sounded not too far from tears. 'I tried so hard to *invest*.'

'Of course.'

'Present-day artists whose work will one day be famous.'

'They'll not be feeling too happy.'

'Some of the lesser-known Victorian painters. They're coming back into vogue.'

'Are they?'

'It will take years to build up another collection. *Years!*'

'You're young enough,' grunted the librarian.

'Don't you care? Don't you even *care*?' The curator's question carried indignation.

'Eh?'

'Aren't you even *concerned*? Aren't you shocked?'

'About your paintings?'

'If not that, about your books?'

'Oh, aye – books. Books and paintings.' The librarian sucked his lips for a moment. Very deliberately, he said, 'Y'see, I have certain values. Certain standards, you might say. I like books – I like reading – otherwise I wouldn't be what I am. But I've reached certain conclusions. Let me explain. Books, my young and earnest friend, are written by people. Good books, popular books, even bad books. All written by people. Men and women with bowels and bladders – just like the rest of us. The same with paintings, unless I'm very much mistaken.

'Now that – as far as *I'm* concerned – makes people a damn sight more important than books. A damn sight more important than paintings, come to that. And people – fully-fledged, paid-up members of the human race – have died in this little lot. Not authors, not writers, not painters, not sculptors . . . *people*. Other people have been injured. It seems possible – even likely – that people will *still* die.'

'Look, I don't see what . . .'

'Bugger the books,' said the librarian, gently. 'Come to that, bugger the pictures. Bugger the statues. I would happily give every book in the library, every painting and statue in your gallery, in exchange for *one* of those lives. In exchange for the certainty that nobody else will die. That the injured will all get well.'

'Oh, agreed. Agreed . . . absolutely.'

'I hope so,' said the librarian, heavily. 'I hope you *do* agree. Because, if you don't, you just might find yourself in a rather tricky situation. Explaining to some wife who's lost her husband – some kid who's lost its father – just how "irreplaceable" your damn paintings *are*. How it will take years to re-build that collection of yours.'

'I – er – I didn't mean to imply . . .'

'You're blinkered, old son.' Sadness gave the librarian's tone a paternal quality. 'Paint, canvas, paper, print, bricks and mortar. That's all you can see. Unimportant things. Trivialities. Stupid things when placed alongside human life. Stop moaning, friend. Stop wailing the place down. You and I . . . we've lost *nothing*.'

14

It was past midday and up on The Tops there was no shelter from the sun. The never-ending breeze was one of nature's more subtle lies. It cooled a little – seemed to take the edge off the scorching discomfort of the high sun – but Parker could feel the tenderness on the bridge of his nose and on his cheeks. Come evening – come morning – the skin would be peeling. Mad dogs and Englishmen . . . and, in particular, detective chief inspectors.

'Where does this path lead to?' asked Hoyle.

'Haggthorpe . . . eventually.' Parker removed his peaked cap and wiped the sweat band with a handkerchief as he added, 'It's a hell of a long walk.'

'For a horse?' Hoyle seemed quite unaware of Parker's discomfort. He said, 'Not a long way for a horse . . . surely?'

'Not for a horse,' agreed Parker, wearily.

'A nice night,' mused Hoyle. 'Light enough to see.'

'Nearly a full moon,' sighed Parker.

'That's what I'm getting at.' Hoyle bent to examine the turf which surfaced the path. Rabbits had nibbled it close-cropped and beneath the green the earth had a rubbery texture. A texture similar to tyre rubber. Hoyle glanced up at Parker, and asked, 'Know much about woodcraft, Parker?'

'No, sir.' Parker scratched the stubble of his embryo

beard. 'I'm not too hot on Fenimore Cooper stuff.'

'No Scout training?' smiled Hoyle.

'No, sir.'

'Nor I.' Hoyle straightened, then continued, 'Common gumption, though . . . eh? A *walking* horse wouldn't make much impression on this stuff. At full gallop, maybe, but not walking.'

'They do it all the time in TV westerns,' observed Parker, drily.

'Eh?'

'A broken twig here, a disturbed leaf there. The posse tracks 'em half-way across America.'

'On films. On television,' agreed Hoyle.

'But not in real life, sir.'

'Not *that* way,' agreed Hoyle. 'But, to an outsider, horses have a strange digestive system. They're forever dropping what gardeners put around their rhubarb.'

'Yes, *sir*,' said Parker without enthusiasm.

Hoyle expanded his theory, and said, 'I can't see any nag walking all the way from Haggthorpe without doing *that*.'

'If – er – if it came from Haggthorpe.'

'Okay. We'll eliminate Haggthorpe for starters. Then, if not Haggthorpe, we'll see where the other paths take us.'

'Just you and me?' Parker stared. 'Just the *two* of us?'

'It's your beat, Parker.'

'Yes, sir – but . . .'

'That beard of yours. Is it sapping your strength?'

'No, sir.' Parker didn't find the sally amusing.

'Is this your first murder enquiry?'

'Yes, sir.'

'Obviously.' Hoyle nodded. 'You'll learn, Parker. It's *not* like it is in detective stories. It's not even like it is in textbooks. Out here a straightforward street-by-street, house-to-house approach isn't possible. A yard-at-a-time, line-abreast search isn't practical . . . the area's too big. What's left is what *we're* doing. Grafting. Working your balls off. And, because this is *your* beat, *your* balls aren't sacrosanct.'

'No, sir.'

'So-o . . . let's walk to Haggthorpe, if necessary.'

It wasn't necessary. Less than a mile farther along the path they found horse droppings.

Hoyle looked almost pleased. He shook out a handkerchief and said, 'Collect the evidence, Parker. Carry it in this. The forensic boys will be delighted to work out what sort of fodder went in at the front end.'

Parker expected the find to satisfy, but it didn't. The walk continued and, after another half mile, they found more horse droppings.

'Do you have a handkerchief?' asked Hoyle.

'Yes, sir.'

'Fine. Use yours for this sample.'

'Sir,' objected Parker in a tired voice, 'if we've *one* sample, surely that's enough for . . .'

'I can't see the same horse crapping twice in so short a time.'

'Oh!'

'And, if it dropped this lot on its way home it's too much of a coincidence for me to accept at first sight. Two horses, Parker. There has to be two horses.'

'If you say so, sir.' Parker fished a handkerchief from his pocket as he spoke and the tone of his voice was that of a man past caring.

'Get it off your chest, Parker,' said Hoyle, grimly.

'Sir?'

'Forget the rank. You obviously feel hard done by. Let's be hearing why.'

'I'm tired. I'm hungry,' complained Parker. 'I haven't been off duty since yesterday. I haven't had a meal since I came *on* duty. I think it's time I had a break but, instead, I'm traipsing around The Tops collecting horse droppings.'

'You'd prefer a deerstalker hat and magnifying glass?'

sneered Hoyle. 'A locked room, perhaps? Some country mansion somewhere, with everybody diving in and out of rooms like characters in a French farce? Is *that* your idea of a murder enquiry?'

'Sir, I appreciate the . . .'

'Nothing!' snapped Hoyle. 'You appreciate *nothing*. You don't even appreciate the luck you've had.'

'Luck?' Parker's eyes widened.

'The horse you saw. *You* weren't supposed to see it. Not a copper. But you *saw* it and you know *when* you saw it, and that's important – something else you don't appreciate. It gave us the best lead we've had so far. It gave *you* that lead.'

'I don't quite see it that way.' Parker spoke slowly, as if choosing his words. 'I'm sorry, sir. I may be dumb, but . . .'

'You're dumb,' agreed Hoyle, but some of the bite had left his tone. He took a deep breath, then added, 'Okay, Parker, you're not a jack. You're a conscientious little wooden-top who drives around this king-sized beat, dutifully making sure nobody poaches his lordship's birds. That's what you are, and that's what you can do to perfection. But what happened last night is in a different league, and you'd be wise to realise that. *And* that it happened here, and to you.

'What we know – what *you* should have worked out – is this.'

Hoyle ticked the points off on his fingers as he continued, 'Point One. She'd been dead some few hours when you found her. The pathologist verifies that, but the absence of blood gave a pointer. She was brought to where you found her and just *before* you found her. That road isn't on a par with Piccadilly Circus, but it's not *that* quiet. Any real length of time and a passing motorist would have spotted the body and yelled the place down.

'Point Two. She was dressed in riding gear and you saw a runaway horse. Gee-gees have a place in the scheme of things. The middle of the night, a good moon, these bridle-paths. It's fair to assume the body was carried to the scene on a nag. Okay, *one* horse would do it. A rider with the body slung across the saddle in front of him. But, if *that*, he had to walk home after the horse bolted. So let's make an educated guess, and plump for *two* horses. One for the rider, one for the body. An altogether more *comfortable* way.

'Point Three . . . assuming two horses. The one that bolted – the one *you* saw – where is it? If it's still missing, the owner won't be keen on reporting its loss. If it's found its way home, the owner will still be sweating. Horses, complete with saddle and harness, tend to be noticed and it *could* have been heading in a direction *we're* interested in.'

'Why not just bring her out in a car, and dump her?' asked Parker. 'Why tool around with horses in the first place?'

'Because,' Hoyle scowled sudden annoyance, 'let's say motor cars have licence plates.'

'They're a bloody sight less obvious than horses at that time of night.'

'But, not on bridle-paths.'

'He wouldn't have *used* the bridle-path,' countered Parker. 'He'd have used the road.'

'A-ah!'

'But of course – as we both agree – *I'm* dumb. A wooden-top who drives around keeping his eyes skinned for poachers.'

'We can't know everything within the first few hours,' muttered Hoyle.

'Not even a *detective*?' Parker's lips moved into a slow, sardonic smile. 'Not even a detective chief *inspector*?'

'Who the hell do you think you're . . .'

'Something about "forgetting rank"?' Parker reminded him gently.

Hoyle's eyes narrowed slightly, and he snapped, 'Right . . . the rank's back in place. Collect those horse droppings and handle them carefully. They could be evidence.'

38

The Assistant Secretary in the Police Department of the Home Office was in urgent telephonic conversation with his opposite number at the Ministry of Defence.

The Home Office man was saying, 'McQuilly's already on his way north.'

'Over-reacting, perhaps?' The MOD man was noted for his ability to use a question with all the skill of an Apaché using a knife.

'The Prime Minister's office wouldn't agree.'

'They rarely do. About anything.'

'You're out-voted, old man. The Northern Ireland crowd are backing us all the way.'

'Do *they* carry weight?'

The HO man allowed a tight smile to touch his mouth as he said, 'Instructions from on high, old man. The Civil Aviation Authority are to be warned off.'

'Just to go through the motions?'

'Not even that. We'll have our own men on the scene.'

'My word! We *are* getting hot around the collar.'

'Check with the top office, old man.'

'Don't think I won't.'

'We'll have a junior Transport Ministry official up there tomorrow morning. He'll be well briefed.'

'Talk a lot, but say little?'

'Old man, he'll say *nothing*. Meanwhile our job is to keep the CAA team out of the playing area.'

Lessford Hospital knew all about what had happened. Since the helicopter had crashed on to the city centre the ambulances had been shuttling in the dead and the injured. The dead were soon disposed of, but the injured seemed to go on forever. The operating tables were busy and half-empty wards were now full to overflowing. The night staff had been called back from their sleep to augment those who had been on duty only a few hours. Surgeons were busy slicing, stitching and amputating. Extra plasma was being rushed in to deal with the sudden increase in the need for blood.

The less glamorous departments had their share in the upsurge of activity. The administrative people were busy cancelling and rearranging appointments; explaining as politely as possible that non-emergency operations had to be postponed and that new times and dates would be given.

It was an incident of 'disaster' proportions and the hospital was responding.

Alva Hoyle was helping in the dispensary. She forced herself to concentrate in order to keep her mind away from a more personal and more agonising heart-break.

Alva's was an unusual role within the hospital personnel. The wife of a detective chief inspector, she had come to accept and tolerate the streak of chauvinism in her husband. She was, therefore, unpaid despite her own PhD and was content to be a superior dogsbody. She assisted in the dispensary. When needed she was equally content to push trolleys along corridors. She lent a hand at making beds. She even trundled the mobile library from ward to ward and made suggestions to bored patients regarding suitable reading. Over the years she had become respected as a willing and uncomplaining extra pair of hands when and where they were needed.

'New hypo needles.' The chief pharmacist slid a loaded key-ring along the bench. 'Nip along to the store, Alva, old darling. A new carton should see us through for a while.'

Alva nodded without taking her eyes from the analgesics she was counting prior to dropping them into a plastic phial.

'And Alva, old darling, no immediate urgency. Take ten. Take twenty. You've been steaming ahead too long without a break. You could use a coffee and doughnut.'

Again, Alva nodded without speaking. She hadn't noticed before – on the other hand, perhaps she *had* noticed but, previously, had been wise enough to ignore the irritation – but today the chief pharmacist's habit of slipping pseudo-transatlantic phraseology into his remarks annoyed her. What the hell was wrong with simple, Anglo-Saxon English? He was a moderately well-educated man, so why the hell not *speak* like one? And, why spice everything up with sprink-lings of 'old darling'? She wasn't *his* 'darling' or ever would be. As for the 'old' bit, *he* was damn near old enough to be her father.

Alva Hoyle was not in a happy mood.

She tightened the screw-top of the phial and placed it ready for collection. She replaced the lid of the container and returned the container to its place on the shelf. Then she picked up the keys and left the dispensary.

As she hurried along the corridors she was aware of the increased activity around her, but it left her untouched. The bustle was there and at times it slowed her progress, but despite being occasionally jostled she was not part of that bustle. Part of her own world was threatening to cave in on her and she was human enough – selfish enough – to be more concerned about *that* than about the greater catastrophe of which the hospital had become a part.

She saw a uniformed figure hurrying towards her and almost before they were within speaking distance Alva swerved slightly and said, 'How's . . . '

'Helen?' The ward sister ended the question. She moistened her lips and continued, 'I was coming to see you. They said you were in the . . . '

'How *is* she?' insisted Alva.

'I'm sorry,' murmured the ward sister, sadly.

'Oh, my God!'

'It was . . . ' The ward sister moved her shoulders in a gesture of defeated resignation. She reached out a hand and touched Alva's arm. 'We rather expected it. We'd have been surprised if she'd lived.'

Alva leaned her shoulders against the wall of the corridor and stared with out-of-focus eyes at the polished floor.

'I . . . ' The ward sister took a deep breath and tried again. 'The doctor – Doctor Shaw – he's with her. He – y'know – he wants to ask you something. A favour, I think. He – he sent me to look for you – before he goes back to Emergency.'

17

'The sort of damn-fool thing she'd get herself mixed up in.' Cossitter sipped at his third whisky. 'She was that kind of an idiot.'

Hobart watched this pint-sized fire-eater and wondered when he and the detective constable could leave. Whether they *should* leave.

He asked, 'Mr Cossitter, is there somebody we can contact?'

'Eh?' Cossitter glared.

'A friend, perhaps? A neighbour?'

'Why the devil should you . . . '

'To sit with you for a while.'

'You want the truth, Hobart?' Cossitter finished the whisky in a single gulp and held out the glass to the DC as he continued, 'I have no friends . . . no real *friends*. And every last one of my neighbours is a pain in the arse.'

The detective constable took the glass and, having

42

received a tiny nod of permission from the detective inspector, he rose to his feet and moved towards the drinks-cabinet.

'We – er – we aren't absolutely sure yet, of course,' murmured Hobart.

'That it's Anthea?'

'We tend to be jumping to certain conclusions, without . . .'

'Great God, man! You're a detective, aren't you?'

'Yes, but . . . '

'One hell of a detective if you can't recognise somebody from a perfectly good photograph.' And, when Hobart didn't answer, Cossitter continued, 'Don't pussyfoot around, inspector. You've asked your questions, you've had your answers, you're free to slope off and find the bastard who did it.' Cossitter took the refilled glass from the DC, touched his lips with the whisky then held the glass within the fingers of both hands and nestled on his lap. He continued talking but the impression was that he didn't give much of a damn whether or not either of the officers heeded what he was saying and his tone was harsher but less aggressive than before.

'You'll walk a damn long way before you bump up against anyone else like me, my friend. A *damn* long way! A long way before you find a man who cared less what other people think of him. It makes for independence, but it doesn't make for popularity. That's what too many people chase – cheap popularity. They yearn to be liked. To be loved. To have their stupid little heads patted like some well-behaved lap-dog. Not me, my friend. Not *me* . . . '

Cossitter paused long enough to bring the glass to his lips then return it to his lap. Hobart figured the intake of booze was having some effect. There was a certain amount of talking for the sake of talking. A mumbling – almost snarling – quality which smacked of self-recrimination. But this *was* a murder enquiry and the search for leads took top priority.

'. . . a cow. A stupid, arrogant cow who thought she could change me. And I married her. I didn't love her – good God, you don't *love* women like that! – but she was the best of the circuit's bad lot and at the time it seemed a good idea. The best driver, the best-looking woman, in bed together . . . officially.'

'The – er – circuit?' said Hobart, gently.

'The racing circuit. Le Mans, Silverstone, Monaco.' Cossitter tasted the whisky. 'You've never heard of me? . . . no, of course you haven't. Hunt, Scheckter, Lauda – but who the hell remembers Cossitter? But I was going to *do* things . . .'

'I'm sorry. It's not my sport.'

'. . . I was the up-and-coming Golden Boy. I was going to out-Fangio Fangio. I was going to make Moss and Clark look like novices. I could have done, too. I had it in me. Not just the speed – any damn fool can shove his foot down and hope for the best – but I had that extra *something*. It can't be taught. It can only be honed and polished. And I had it. To know, instinctively, the exact line of a corner. The split second when the man in front's concentration *has* to be elsewhere and you can slip past him. How to close the gate on the man coming up behind. I knew these things. Knew them the moment I first wedged myself into a cockpit and felt that wheel vibrating under my hands. I was the up-and-coming king. All I needed was the right car, and I was *getting* the right cars . . .'

18

'A bomb,' insisted Flensing.

'Sit down, chief superintendent.' Gilliant waved Flensing to a chair. Then, when the offer was accepted, 'We'll know. When the experts can get in there and make an examination, we'll know.'

Flensing looked a very tired man. He also looked bruised. A graze on his right cheek was evidence of physical bruising, and his hands, face and clothes were grubby and dust-streaked. His hair was matted and there was a scorch mark on the cuff of his jacket.

But the bruised look went deeper than immediate externals. It was there in the droop of the shoulders, the lines on the face and the haggardness of the eyes. He was a man who'd taken a mental and an emotional beating. He'd been at the library and the art gallery too long, had witnessed too much and had plunged into a depth of helplessness from which he would take long to recover.

Gilliant saw it and was saddened. Even Harris saw it . . . but Harris wasn't the type to accept the burdens of other men.

In a weary voice, Flensing said, 'Chief constable, there's nothing wrong with my hearing. Two. Two different *kinds* of explosion. The second was the helicopter going up, but the first was a *bomb*.'

Gilliant nodded. It was not the nod of a man agreeing with an assessment. It was merely a sign that he understood what was being said.

'If there was a bomb . . .' began Harris.

'There *was* a bomb.'

'Express an opinion, Flensing,' growled Harris. 'Don't be so bloody *sure*. You'll only look a bigger fool if you're wrong.'

'How many dead?' Flensing's tone changed. It became hard and tight.

'Eighteen at the last count.'

'Eighteen. And, if the hospital people are to be believed, we'll be lucky if the final tally doesn't top the twenty mark. And you, Harris, sit on your rump *counting*!'

'At the present moment it's tagged "disaster". Until we have something specific . . .'

'Hell's teeth, I *know*.'

45

'Go home, chief superintendent,' said Gilliant, gently. 'If it's what you say it is we'll find proof. Then, it's yours – all yours. That's a promise. I'll not . . .'

'Eighteen,' choked Flensing. He seemed not to have heard Gilliant. 'Eighteen, and more than twice that number badly injured. *Badly* injured. Burned to hell. Broken. I helped pull some of the poor devils clear.' He paused long enough to take three deep sighs. It was an effort, but he regained control of himself. In a quieter but more controlled voice he added, 'It wasn't easy, sir.'

'Of course not.'

'I can't remember living through a worse few hours.'

'Rough,' agreed Gilliant, gently.

Harris said, 'We're expected to take the rough times without cracking up.'

'But not *that* rough.'

'Yes – *that* rough.' Harris moved his lips in what might have been a half-smile of contempt. 'It's expected of us, Flensing. More. It's bloody-well *demanded* of us. It's the bit they don't mention in the recruiting ads. What the hell we do in private – however many tears we spill in the beer behind locked doors – when a thing like this happens we play PC Plod, and like it. If you haven't yet realised *that* you've led a very sheltered life. It's tough, it's hard, it's a damn sight more hairy than escorting kids across a busy road . . . but *that*, detective chief superintendent, is the name of the game.'

'I'm sorry,' muttered Flensing.

'Don't be – not here.' Then, after a pause, Gilliant added, 'Let's see what we've got.'

'A bomb. Nothing will convince me it wasn't a . . .'

' . . . a bomb.' Gilliant ended the sentence for him, then continued, 'Fine. For the moment – as a starting point, if you like – we'll accept that proposition. A bomb planted in a helicopter. The blazing helicopter crashes into the centre of a city – into the centre of Lessford – and we have what amounts to a major disaster on our hands. Where does that leave us?'

Gilliant paused to stare at the dirt-streaked face of the detective chief superintendent.

Harris contributed, 'It's the age we live in, Flensing. It's the modern dimension of murder. Not the pokey killing you have on The Tops.'

'She's no less dead,' countered Flensing.

Before the assistant chief constable (crime) could answer, Gilliant said, 'Dublin, Belfast – even London – they've grown to accept it. It's reached Birmingham. It's moving north.'

Harris said, 'Into our neck of the woods, Flensing. It *had* to come. The anti-terrorist crowd are making things too hot for 'em around the old targets.'

'You think terrorists?' Flensing's question carried what could only be described as hopeful doubt.

'For Christ's sake!' muttered Harris.

'I think it possible,' said Gilliant. 'If there was a bomb . . .'

'There *was* a bomb.'

'In that case, terrorism seems likely.'

'More than bloody "likely",' growled Harris.

Flensing felt in his jacket pocket and located a packet of cigarettes. The truth was the cigarettes weren't there to be smoked. For more than a month they'd represented Flensing's latest fight to break the habit. Five cigarettes left in a packet which had originally held twenty and, when the urge had been almost unbearable, he'd opened the packet to glare defiance at the five cigarettes and mentally stormed against his own weak will-power in the face of the pseudo-satisfaction offered by five elongated cylinders of shredded tobacco leaf.

This time he needed a cigarette badly. This time he made no effort to resist the temptation.

Having taken a cigarette from the packet and placed it between his lips, Flensing returned the packet and began patting his pockets for matches he knew weren't there.

Gilliant smiled understanding and, from his own pocket, produced a lighter which he thumbed into flame and held out for the detective chief superintendent.

'Thanks.' Flensing touched the tip of the cigarette into the flame before fumbling in his pockets to find the packet of cigarettes once more. 'Sorry, I should have offered you . . . '

'Not for the moment.'

Flensing drew the first deep inhalation and immediately doubled up in a fit of coughing. He regained control of his breathing and for a moment stared at the cigarette between his fingers as if unable to believe that his lungs no longer accepted tobacco smoke without protest.

Gilliant waited a moment, then said, 'Let's start with the assumption we're dealing with terrorists. Where does that leave us?'

'If terrorists . . . ' Flensing raised the cigarette to his lips for a second tentative inhalation. This time he drew less deeply and blew a tiny scarf of smoke before he continued. 'If terrorists, I think they'd have notified us. Or, am I wrong? Would they?'

'Maybe.' In the privacy of his own office and in the company of close colleagues Gilliant could admit of some ignorance. 'As I see things, it varies. Sometimes they give warning before it happens . . . whatever "it" is. Sometimes they lay claim immediately afterwards. Sometimes more than one lot claim to be responsible. Sometimes . . . nothing.'

'They're lunatics,' said Harris, sourly. 'So are the clowns who supposedly understand 'em. They don't tell us a damn thing until it's too late.'

'Some sort of password, as proof it isn't a hoax,' murmured Flensing. 'Some sort of identifying phrase.'

'If so, nobody's notified *this* office.'

'Cloak-and-dagger stuff,' complained Harris. 'A damn sight too much up-the-sleeve crap.'

'Of necessity, Mr Harris,' sighed Gilliant. He cupped his

chin and rubbed a cheek with the tips of his fingers as he continued, '*If* terrorists, common sense suggests they don't want to end up in the net. They want to get back to base – wherever "base" is – before they make any claims.'

Flensing muttered, 'It's a nonsense. I've never been able to fully understand it. Not even from a distance. But *now*! It's not revenge. Nobody takes revenge out of strangers . . .'

'If they're mad enough,' grunted Harris.

' . . . It's not hatred. Damnation, they don't even *know* the eighteen they've killed today, so they can't hate them. There's no reason. Good God, there's just no *reason*!'

'They don't need what you or I would call a "reason", Flensing,' said Gilliant, sadly. 'The killing itself is reason enough. Not *who* gets killed. The killing makes the point they want to make. That they're still around. That they're still in business.'

19

It was past two o'clock and, out on The Tops, a brazen sun was gradually defeating the continuous cool of the breeze. It would get hotter within the next two to three hours. It always did on days like this. The rolling distances seemed to shimmer as the sun sucked moisture from the low vegetation, and it needed little imagination to see how, without the rains of autumn and the blizzards of winter, such a place could turn into a desert.

Both Motor Patrol units had been relieved and now new officers were waving passing vehicles to a halt to ask drivers and passengers when they'd last used the road. Reeve had sought what shade he could in his car, with all windows rolled down.

It was (Reeve decided) monumentally boring. Boring and bloody hot. Murder enquiries (as Reeve understood things) were wild and whirling affairs. Clip-boards by the score, sore knuckles from knocking on doors, laryngitis from asking the same set of questions over and over again. That was the general impression.

Not that Reeve *knew*, not from personal experience, that is. His had been a very pedestrian police career. He'd kept his nose clean, of course; the odd Swine Fever panic here, a touch of Domestic Disturbance there with the occasional nicking of some light-fingered local who lacked the basic gumption to lift something without bragging about it to half the neighbourhood. But no trees uprooted by request. No ball-of-fire antics.

He'd made sergeant because . . . We-ell, because there'd been a *vacancy*. As daft as *that*. A sergeant had retired and the powers-that-be had looked around for a replacement. To Reeve's personal knowledge four coppers had turned down the promotion before it had been offered to *him*. Presumably the other four had had their eyes on greater things. Making a name for themselves. Hitting the headlines.

Not so Reeve. Reeve had accepted the chevrons with a sigh of relief. Umpteen square miles of sod-all equated with a quiet life and an eventual pension, and no man could ask for more than that.

He saw Hoyle and Parker approaching through the carpet of heather. They both looked knackered – and small wonder in this heat – and Parker was carrying two knotted handkerchiefs. One in each hand. Like a navvy carrying his lunch. That bloody Constable Parker would have to be told. Traipsing around looking like a latter-day Dick Whittington could give the section a bad name. It could result in *him* (Reeve) being at the receiving end of a rollicking – which would never do.

Reeve climbed from the car, ran a finger around the collar of his soaked shirt, touched his tie, straightened his helmet and waited.

What Reeve expected is not known. What he *got* was both barrels from a very irate Hoyle.

'Where the hell *is* everybody?'

'Sir?' Reeve tended to be flabbergasted at the unexpected explosion.

'The coppers,' roared Hoyle. 'The bobbies, the wooden-tops, the fuzz. The police officers, sergeant. Where the hell *are* they all? Has somebody called an unexpected national strike of law-enforcement personnel?'

'Well – no, sir – but . . . ' Reeve flapped his arms, helplessly.

'But *what*?'

'There's two there.' Reeve pointed. 'And two there. Four – and myself. Five. We're – er – stopping all cars . . . '

'*Five!*'

'They've – they've gone home, sir. They've finished. Done what they came to do. The photographers, and the . . . '

'Five,' repeated Hoyle, and this time in a whisper as if he daren't allow himself freedom of complete expression. He took a deep breath, then said, 'Five. Five blasted coppers, all tucked away in their comfortable motor cars. All busy doing sweet F.A. All drawing a damn good wage for doing bugger-all – and this is the centre of a murder enquiry.'

'The – er – the centre, sir?' Reeve was puzzled.

'This is where it happened, sergeant. Or doesn't your memory stretch that far back?'

'Oh yes, sir. But . . . '

'And there was some talk of a finger search.'

'Oh!'

'A finger search, sergeant.' Hoyle was winding himself up again. 'D'you know what a finger search is?'

'Er – yes, sir. But . . . '

'It means coppers – as many coppers as you can get your hands on – down on their hands and knees. Looking. Using their eyes. Inch at a time – foot at a time – seeking whatever is there that shouldn't *be* there.'

'Er – yes, sir. But . . . '

'A cigarette end, a used match, a thrown-away sweet wrapper. Evidence, sergeant. Evidence!'

'Horse apples,' murmured Parker.

'What?' Hoyle whirled on the weary constable and stared his suspicion.

'Horse apples, sir,' said Parker with exaggerated innocence. He moved the two knotted handkerchiefs. 'What we've been collecting. Evidence.'

'Ah!' For a moment Hoyle's eyes narrowed with mistrust, then he returned his attention to Reeve. 'Exactly, sergeant. Evidence, as Parker says. Great God, man, you don't think sitting here getting a sun-tan will trace the murderer, do you?'

'No, sir. But . . .'

'I expected to find men here, waiting. Enough men to form a close-scrutiny-search detail. Instead, I find two bloody squad cars checking on people who know damn-all, and you sunning yourself like a tart on the Costa Brava.'

'The helicopter, sir,' gasped Reeve.

'I don't expect *brains* in this neck of the woods. I don't expect . . .' Hoyle closed his mouth, then said, 'The what?'

'The – er – the helicopter,' stammered Reeve.

'*What* bloody helicopter?'

'The one that's crashed on Lessford.'

'I don't know what the devil you're . . .'

'Lessford Headquarters called all the men in, sir. Just me and a couple of Motor Patrol units to stay here. Those were the orders, sir.'

'From Lessford Headquarters?' Hoyle seemed suddenly to run out of steam.

'From Mr Harris, sir.'

'Oh!'

Everybody kept a straight face. Hoyle felt like performing an immediate operation on Reeve's throat, Dracula-style. Parker's inside was one huge grin. Reeve felt hard done by, but realised he'd somehow backed a detective chief inspector down a hole. Each felt both aggrieved and, in some way, triumphant. It was a curious and disconcerting feeling; rather

52

like that of a high-wire walker who, looking down, suddenly realises that somebody has removed the safety net.

Therefore everybody kept a straight face.

20

It can be argued that hospitals are dangerous places. People die in hospitals. Of necessity, then, hospital mortuaries tend towards spaciousness. The mortuary at Lessford Hospital was, indeed, large but it needed every square inch at its disposal. It had never seen such activity. Eighteen extra bodies – nineteen, counting the murdered girl – and they all had to be stripped, cleaned up and provisionally identified prior to joining the queue for the pathologist's table.

'I call them "guests",' said the mortuary attendant.

The sergeant looked up from his slightly gruesome task.

'"Guests",' repeated the attendant. 'Those who don't die in hospital. That's what I call them.'

'Oh!'

'It sounds less – y'know – formal.'

'You can hang a "No Vacancies" sign on the door,' grunted the sergeant.

Some trick of acoustics gave the room an eerie, hollow sound. It was a tiled box with built-in cabinets and a stainless steel operating table with runnels leading to a wide-mouthed central drain. It was a very *functional* place. Everything was fixed and firm. Nothing vibrated. Yet this weird half-echo persisted. It went with the smell of clinical cleanliness and death. It nudged some primeval fear and triggered a subconscious moistening of the lips.

The sergeant doing duty as coroner's officer was within a year of retirement. He was shockproof; he'd seen everything and heard everything and his dry, caustic speech was an outward evidence of his impassiveness. He was in his shirt sleeves and handling the cadavers much as a master butcher might handle sides of beef.

His companion, the hospital mortuary attendant, was of about the same age but of a different temperament. He was overtly, and painfully, religious; a 'born again' Christian whose Maker scowled messianic disapproval at all things earthy and all remarks sardonic.

The sergeant growled, 'Move over, you awkward sod,' as he struggled to remove the underpants from a portly corpse.

'Please have respect, sergeant,' said the attendant, disapprovingly.

'You think he might hear?'

'He's somebody's loved one.'

'Aye. With a belly like this she's not a bad cook, either.'

'When *your* time comes . . . ' began the attendant.

'When *my* time comes,' interrupted the sergeant, 'I shall be like laddo, here. The massed bands of the Brigade of Guards can crack on at full blast. I'll be well past hearing and well past caring.'

There followed a silence. The attendant looked hurt rather than shocked. From some celestial skylight the soul of the dead man was watching; what had once housed that soul was being mocked and although the indigestions and headaches which had been part of that inhabitation were now a thing of the past the whole had once included what the sergeant was now treating with complete irreverence. It wasn't nice. It wasn't *right*.

The sergeant didn't give a damn. He had a job to do. It was a thankless job and a tasteless job, but he'd had worse. And the only thing that *really* mattered was the monthly pay cheque.

In all but four cases provisional identification had been made. Wallets, diaries, old letters, address books, cheque books. There'd been *something*. And, having emptied all pockets, all handbags, all brief-cases – having made an educated guess at the name of the victim – the contents of the handbag, the pocket and/or the brief-case were placed in a plastic bag along with watches, rings and other jewellery before the corpse was stripped mother-naked and the clothes folded and also placed in the plastic bag. A name tag was fixed to the plastic bag and another name tag was tied to the big toe of the body. Then, the body was draped in a white sheet to await the attention of the pathologist.

It was all very efficient, all very necessary and all very cold-blooded. Except, of course, when the injuries were horrific enough to make the sergeant hesitate for a moment. Then, certain puke-making requirements were called for. They were performed.

Because even death does not bring complete obscurity. A corpse claims the final dignity of an identity, and here eighteen separate identities had to be established before inquests could be held. Eighteen times some person – some 'next of kin' – had to look down at a lifeless face and make formal recognition.

Therefore, basic decency meant that the muck and carnage of violent death had to be sponged away before identification was finally established. But that would come later in the assembly-line-like duties of the sergeant and the mortuary attendant.

Meanwhile the sergeant held up a thin bundle of paste-boards.

'These?' he asked.

'Where are they from?'

'This one's wallet.' The sergeant had moved from the stout cadaver and was dealing with the body of a middle-aged man in a torn and scorched suit which, nevertheless, gave the appearance of being more expensive than mere off-the-peg. 'Photographs. Six of 'em.'

'What are you getting at?' The mortuary attendant looked puzzled. 'You know perfectly well they have to be . . . .'

'He's a married man.' The sergeant cut into the attendant's

obvious remark. 'Joint bank account. Mister and missus. And there's some family snapshots by the look of things.'

'In that case . . .'

'These.' The sergeant flipped a fingernail through the bundle in his hand. 'Dirty pictures. *Very* dirty pictures. Some of the juiciest I've ever seen.'

'Oh!'

'Of course, his wife might be one of these modern, broad-minded types. You read about 'em sometimes.'

'Ah!'

'You're the lad with all the moral scruples,' explained the sergeant. 'Me? I'd sling 'em into the nearest furnace, but you're setting the pace.'

'Well – er . . .'

'But of course burning 'em amounts to nicking 'em and I'm wondering what that flash conscience of yours has to say about filching from a corpse.'

21

In the corridors of Whitehall and in the offices of Westminster a great fiction was being played out. It was the Official Ignorance game. Orders were passed by word of mouth. Instructions were given by telephone. But nothing was put in writing and nobody signed anything.

The Prime Minister didn't know. The Home Secretary didn't know. The Defence Minister, the Minister of Transport and Aviation and the Minister in charge of Northern Ireland were all equally innocent.

Had they known – had they *officially* known – their respective outraged amazements would have cut no ice when (and if) some stroppy opposition back-bencher had sniffed something out and asked awkward questions.

Igornance, therefore, equated with innocence.

Permanent Under Secretaries of State and Deputy Under Secretaries of State were also unaware. At Space House,

Kingsway, the top officials of the Civil Aviation Authority were just as much in the dark.

The depth of this layer of artless bewilderment was truly amazing.

Everybody was interested, but nobody *knew*.

The hell they didn't know.

22

' . . . you can't drive without legs,' said Cossitter. 'That's something the stupid bitch could never accept. I hadn't much choice. It was that or a blasted coffin. A straight "or else" situation. I was lucky, really. That's what everybody told me. Lucky! It could have been that *and* a coffin.' Cossitter downed the last of the whisky and held out the glass for the DC to collect. He muttered, 'But she could have *tried*, eh? Dammit, she could have tried. She could have . . . '

'Your daughter,' murmured Hobart.

'Eh?'

'Anthea.' Hobart signalled with his eyes and the DC stood up to play barman once more. Hobart continued, 'Cossitter, we think your daughter's been murdered. That's why we're here.'

'I know why you're here.' Booze slurred the words slightly. 'You're here because . . . '

'It's a murder enquiry.' A certain grimness entered Hobart's tone. 'A young woman's been stabbed to death. We think the dead woman might be your daughter. We've been as careful – as gentle – as possible so far, but . . . '

'Oh, it's my daughter, all right.' Cossitter waved his arms a little. 'It's Anthea. She was *born* for it. She was damn-well *born* to have her stupid throat cut.'

'I didn't say she'd had her . . . '

'Damn her! Damn and blast her to hell! She was *born* for it.'

When he broke it was like glass splintering under an excess

57

of pressure. No warning. No obvious strain. He merely folded forward in the chair, with his artificial legs rigidly out at a narrow V in front of him, and the emotional pain made him howl quietly like an animal with a terrible wound. His arms hung limp alongside the mechanical thighs and his shoulders shook as the sobs ripped their way through his shattered body.

The DC breathed, 'Oh, my Christ!' and replaced the top of the whisky bottle. He looked at Hobart for guidance.

'Stay with him,' said Hobart, gently. 'Don't offer him comfort – that's a waste of time. Let him cry himself out. No more questions for the moment, and no more whisky. Just stay with him and make sure he doesn't do anything silly.'

The DC nodded and returned to his chair.

'For the moment, he's your responsibility.' Hobart stood up. 'I'll have a detective sergeant out – probably with a policewoman – as soon as I can. But, for the moment, this end of the enquiry is in your hands.'

23

Harris didn't like Roper. He wasn't crazy about McQuilly, come to that, but McQuilly held the rank of police commander (presumably in one of the fancy 'C' departments of the Met) and even away from his home turf a commander could put thorns and thistles in the path of a mere ACC. McQuilly, therefore, had to be tolerated.

Roper, on the other hand, was too cocky by half. Roper was a mere detective sergeant and he had far too much yap for his rank. Nor did he *look* like a copper – discounting the pantomime variety. On principle Harris disapproved of bandit moustaches and shoulder-length hair. Harris's was a strictly short-back-and-sides-clean-shaven mentality. Roper's style of crap was fine for Yankee TV cops who raced around with shoulder artillery. British bobbies – uniformed or plain-clothes – didn't prance around looking like refugees from a third-rate production of *The Student Prince*.

They were in Gilliant's office. Four of them. Gilliant, Harris, McQuilly and Roper. The last two had arrived from The Big City and (or so it seemed) they were there to slam the shutters on what had happened in Lessford earlier in the day.

Roper was saying, 'He handles shit . . . '

'He does *not*.' Harris's voice was flat and disapproving. 'In this police district he handles heroin.'

Roper's brows knitted and he stared at the assistant chief constable in puzzlement.

'I know all the words,' explained Harris. '"Shit", "Horse", "Junk", "Smack", "Skag" – maybe a few more they've invented recently – but in *this* area we call a spade a spade. Heroin is what you're talking about, sergeant. Call it that, and we'll all be happy.'

'Yes, *sir*,' said Roper, heavily.

McQuilly glanced at Gilliant and tiny muscles at the corners of Gilliant's mouth twitched slightly, as if holding back an urge to grin.

Gilliant said, 'Go on, sergeant.'

'Heroin,' continued Roper, with slight emphasis. 'He handles heroin in large quantities.'

Why a mere detective sergeant was in on the act was something Harris couldn't fathom. And, if a sergeant *was* necessary, why in hell one who wore a shirt open to the navel, a leather waistcoat, faded jeans and calf-length cowboy boots? Such apparitions did not belong in the company of police commanders, chief constables and assistant chief constables. There was a basic dignity due to the damn job. There was even more of a dignity due to this office – a chief constable's office. The books which lined the walls were, in all conscience, musty enough – they dealt with enough garbage, and half the authors didn't know what the hell practical bobbying boiled down to – but they were all *law* books and any man claiming that office as his personal nesting place deserved the courtesy of proper dress and decent conduct.

The truth was, of course, that the externals were just that – externals – and not the real reason for Harris's dislike of the London-based detective sergeant. The dislike was based more upon alchemy than it was on logic or reason. It happens, sometimes. There is an immediate antagonism almost amounting to hatred. Romantics might be tempted to describe it as the reverse side of the love-at-first-sight experience. Anthropologists, zoologists, psychologists and the like might use more technical language and equate Harris's feelings with that of the monarch about to be deposed or a herd-leader sensing a rival for his position of power. But, whatever it was, it was there and it had little to do with Roper's choice of clothes or the manner of his facial hair. Enough that it was excuse, and more, for Harris to listen to what was being said with a scowl of disapproval.

'There was a clamp-down,' continued Roper. 'One hell of a clamp-down. But even The Syndicate – as it now likes to call itself – couldn't pull a complete squeeze. Too many Johnny-come-lately drug bosses working freelance. Too many outlets. Above all, too many hooked on the stuff.'

Harris was about to say something, but McQuilly cut in with, 'Tell the whole story, sergeant. We have to justify our reason for being here, and I think Mr Gilliant might be interested.'

'There was a split in what had once been the Mafia,' said Roper. 'In the old days it couldn't have happened. The links were too strong. But, this time, the Italian end wouldn't play ball. Kids in Southern Italy didn't go to fancy schools. They kept clear of dope because they couldn't afford the stuff. The Mediterranean dons could control their families and didn't give a damn about their penthouse brothers. They enjoyed power, and power needed money, and the fastest way to get rich and stay rich was on the drug train.'

'Clever,' sneered Harris. 'Not to say involved.'

'Involved.' Roper nodded. 'Yeah . . . involved. When people from the American Mafia, from the Italian police, from the Federal Drug Enforcement Agency and even from the United Nations talk behind closed doors – when they work out a combined strategy to blow the Italian Mafia off the face of the earth – I'd call that involved, assistant chief constable. You saw it happen. You read about it in the newspapers. The shootings. The raids. The purpose-built courthouse complete with cages for the scores of bastards who once thought themselves untouchable. As you say . . . involved. It rubbed the corners off the Golden Triangle. The Mediterranean stopped being the world's drug centre. These days, Rotterdam. And, another switch. Drugs aren't only on offer for kicks. These days, drugs are a weapon favoured by terrorists . . .'

24

By late afternoon the media were hunting around for new words and new phrases with which to tighten their grip on the story. National, regional and local radio teams had already pushed their microphones into the faces of people still suffering from shock. Mobile TV units sought official 'confirmation' of their own speculative conclusions.

But nobody confirmed and nobody denied.

'The names of the dead and injured will not be released until the next-of-kin have been informed.'

Nevertheless, it was a great story. It had everything. The crashed helicopter, the wrecked buildings and the fire provided the violence. The dead, the injured and the as-yet-unnamed bereaved took care of the 'human interest'. The evening newspapers held space for last-minute reports and the morning dailies urged their reporters to find some new angle before the 10 p.m. deadline.

The paucity of hard facts presented no problem. Figures were plucked out of thin air and given false credibility. Wild guesses were pumped up until they had the appearance of firm evidence.

Meanwhile, the body of a murdered woman had been found on The Tops . . . but who cared?

25

' . . . Dope has a new use, these days,' concluded Roper.

'Mexico,' rumbled Harris. Dammit, he wasn't about to let this jumped-up Met sergeant flash his know-how around without putting up *some* show of resistance. 'From what I hear, the latest star ratings put Mexico and Colombia on top of the drug league.'

'The "Families",' smiled Roper. 'Some degree of self-promotion, we think. If you can't be famous, try for some degree of notoriety. In other words, for "Godfathers" read "Families".' Roper touched his moustache with the tip of a finger and earned himself a slight curl of Harris's lip.

'Mexico,' he continued, 'exports heroin. By world standards, not a lot. Not even enough to meet the demand of the American junkies. Not *nearly* enough. The bulk of heroin, in all its forms – legal and illegal – now comes from India and Pakistan. With a nice little top-up from Afghanistan. From there, most of the illegal stuff travels to Rotterdam. From *there* . . . anywhere. As far as this country's concerned, a short trip across the North Sea and people are waiting for it. South coast, east coast. In bulk. In penny numbers. It arrives.'

'All neat and tidy,' muttered Harris.

'Not neat. Not even tidy.' McQuilly gave the impression of aligning himself alongside his sergeant. It wasn't a rescue operation, but it *was* a deliberate tipping of the scales until the balance of rank became more equal. His voice was soft and drawling. It was the sort of voice which had to be *listened* to.

'How many dead, today?' asked McQuilly.

'Eighteen, so far.' Gilliant answered the question. 'I'm told more might die before the night's out. Some are in intensive care.'

'Eighteen dead,' mused McQuilly. 'That's a high price to pay for keeping one man alive – wouldn't you say?'

26

Hobart felt aggrieved. It was, when all was said and done, a murder enquiry. Short of face-to-face confrontation with the corpse he *had* established the identity of the victim. To some degree – indeed, to a great degree – he'd discovered that the dead woman was one of those people literally *born* to be murdered. In short, and in view of the fact that the murder was less than a day old, his personal line of enquiry was moving along at an unusual rate of knots.

But (or so it seemed) nobody wanted to know.

Beechwood Brook DHQ was reduced to skeleton coverage. The whole division had been denuded of spare officers. The helicopter crash at Lessford had drawn coppers towards it like so many iron filings being pulled towards a magnet.

'We need some men,' he complained.

The lonely detective sergeant at Beechwood Brook CID Office nodded sympathetically.

'You, for example,' amplified Hobart.

'Not me, squire,' said the DS, glumly. 'Orders from on high. I'm to sit tight till further notice, catching whatever spare crime the division has to offer.'

'This is ridiculous.' Hobart folded himself into a spare chair. 'You, me and a detective constable. A *murder* enquiry! What the blazes can *we* do?'

'You and a detective constable,' corrected the DS. 'I'm

glued on my fanny in this office, hoping to God we stay in the milk bottle league.'

'Not even the detective constable,' sighed Hobart. 'He has a full-time job holding Cossitter's hand.'

'Hercule Poirot could do it,' grinned the DS. 'Shuffle the old grey cells around a bit, twirl the old moustache . . .'

'Sergeant, this isn't funny,' interrupted Hobart, wearily. 'We live in an age of forensic miracles. Personal radios, computers, laser-beam fingerprint identification. There's a top-rank crime been committed out there at the back of beyond. On paper we should have enough jacks and flatfeet available for over-kill. Instead, and because some lunatic doesn't know how to drive a helicopter, we have one ageing detective inspector who was dragged from his bed in the small hours and hasn't yet had a substantial meal. That is *not* funny, sergeant.'

'Sod 'em all, squire,' suggested the DS. 'Eat.'

'That,' said Hobart, 'is the first constructive suggestion I've heard all day.'

27

Hoyle, too, had decided to take a short break from the graft of policing. The trudge across the dusty heat of The Tops had made him feel both grubby and sweaty and he was soaking the tiredness from his body when his wife arrived home. He heard the door of the house open and close. He called and she answered. He heard her climb the stairs and if for a moment the thought crossed his mind that her steps were slower than usual it was followed by the realisation that the hospital must have had a busy day as a result of the crashed helicopter. Like himself, she'd be tired. Like himself, a good soak would work wonders.

Nor did he comprehend her misery when she entered the bathroom still wearing the lightweight mac from outdoors, nor when she lowered herself slowly on to the side of the bath.

'A hard day?' He smiled as he asked the question.

The smile melted and was replaced by a look of concerned puzzlement as the expression on his wife's face registered.

'Sweetheart, what's . . .'

'Helen's dead.'

The two words dropped like ice pellets into the damp warmth of the bathroom.

'What the . . .'

'She died early this afternoon.'

'But – but . . . ' The sudded water of the bath rippled and splashed as Hoyle moved his hands in meaningless gesticulations. 'Ralph. I was with him this morning. He'd have mentioned something if . . .'

'He doesn't know.' She stood up and paced backwards and forwards as she continued speaking. 'Of *course* he doesn't know. How could he? The medics didn't find the bug until yesterday and she swore everybody to silence. She didn't want to worry him. That's what she said. She didn't want to . . .'

'What bug?'

'The iron lung she's lived in ever since we met her.' The words were without modulation. Without emotion. It was as if she daren't inject her conversation with the misery she was keeping under control in case the misery took over. 'She needed that damn contraption to breathe. To *breathe*, for God's sake! The simple process of inhalation and exhalation. *We* do it all the time without thinking. Without being conscious of it. She needed a *machine* to do it for her. What sort of life . . .'

'How the hell can some bug . . .'

'Yesterday. Only *yesterday*. This bronchial thing took over.'

'What "bronchial thing"?'

'Some sort of bronchial disease – some sort of pulmonary

65

embolism – and she couldn't fight it. You need lungs – ordinary working lungs – to fight a thing like that.'

'Sweet Jesus!'

'In a hospital. Surrounded by all the gadgetry of modern medicine. With all the fancy drugs ready to hand. And – and – she just stops breathing.' Alva Hoyle halted her pacing and bent her head forward until it touched the damp surface of the tiled wall. Then, she straightened and turned. She choked, 'That's what happened, David. That's the lousy trick life played on her. Helen. Ralph's Helen. *My* Helen.'

'*Our* Helen.' He'd stepped from the bath and wrapped a king-sized towel around his soaking body. He held out his arms and she moved into them, buried her face into his shoulder and wept. After a few moments, she sobbed, 'How can we tell him, David? What words can we use?'

'You said *we'd* do it?' And, when he felt the tiny nod, he added, 'Of course. We're his friends. We're the people who *should*.'

28

McQuilly had a personality – a charismatic 'presence' – which had no need of outward trappings. Gilliant realised this and eventually, albeit with some reluctance, so did Harris. This police commander from some hole-in-the-corner London law-enforcement department was not a creature to be lightly dismissed. The voice was gentle and educated and the slight drawl more than hinted at public school and university. A *good* public school and one of the Oxbridge seats of learning. The certainty was there; the grasp of facts and the ability to reduce those facts into a single line of thought wrapped tightly around a core of irrefutable logic. It could have sounded like a lecture – even a sermon – but the subtle modulations of the telling kept the attention of his listeners and, while McQuilly talked, Gilliant rose from his chair, walked to a corner cabinet and poured four glasses of moderately good sherry.

The subject was the poppy – the genus Papaver – one of the commonest of nature's wild flowers. Not the Field Poppy – the Flanders Poppy – the Papaver Rhoeas, but the Purple Poppy – the Papaver Somniferum.

' . . . although they have this in common. They're almost weeds. They both produce seeds by the thousand and the seeds can lie dormant in the soil for years and still survive . . .'

A curse or a blessing? The thickened juice from the bud is opium and from opium comes narcotics, sedatives and even emetics. Morphine, narcotine, codeine, narceine, thebaine and anarcotine.

And heroin is a comparatively simple derivative of morphine.

' . . . it follows, therefore, that all this burning of poppy crops is little more than a cosmetic exercise. A publicity stunt. The experts know the truth of it. They're only burning part of *this* year's crop. It will be back next year. Self-sown and perhaps even better for burning . . .'

Heroin, morphine and cocaine. The unholy trio of drug abuse. All can be injected. Heroin can be heated and the 'dragon' can be 'chased' by inhaling the smoke given off. The white powder of cocaine can be sniffed and fools seeking bigger and more lethal kicks go for a shorter life by taking heroin and cocaine together. 'Speedball', 'Hot and Cold' or 'H and C'.

The slang and the permutations change with each season.

' . . . the truth is that the basic economies of some Third World countries are based on the mass production of opium. Some of it for genuine medical purposes. Some for the illegal market. The lines are blurred. The Nelson's eye technique comes in for a lot of mileage. And who can blame them? When you're poor you don't give too much of a damn about where the money comes from . . .'

Gilliant handed round the drinks, then returned to his chair. McQuilly and the sergeant nodded their thanks and moistened their lips. Harris gulped half his glassful in a single swallow, wondered whether the tax- and ratepayers would enthuse about their cash being spent on booze . . . then decided it could be spent on less important things.

McQuilly continued talking. About heroin. About morphine. About people committing suicide without even being aware of what they were doing.

' . . . the Vietcong showed the world how to use drug addiction as a weapon of war. Johnson threw the troops in by the tens of thousands and heroin was waiting for them. They were fed up and far from home, so they accepted it.

'In the long term it was more effective than all the B-52 bombers. The sophisticated equipment on the ground was useless. The men either wouldn't use it or *couldn't* use it. A ragbag army of guerrilla fighters, but with the help of the poppy they plucked the feathers from the American eagle.

'And, of course, every other terrorist outfit in the world saw the sense of it. The simplicity of it. You don't need bombs, you don't need battalions, you don't even need bullets. All you need is dope and enough fools on the other side to take it . . . '

29

'What the devil are *you* doing at home?'

Detective Inspector Clarence Hobart was hungry. He was also a mite weary of apparently carrying the full weight of a murder enquiry across his own aching shoulders. He neither held the rank nor collected the salary for that degree of responsibility.

He'd nipped home for a quick meal, opened the door of the house and immediately been confronted by his son, Morgan, apparently returning to the ground floor from the bedroom area.

Morgan tried a slightly embarrassed smile for size, but it didn't fit.

'Well?' demanded Hobart, as he closed the door on the outside world.

'I'm – er . . . ' Once more the quick smile didn't quite fit. 'I'm *here*.'

'Which is where you *shouldn't* be. You should be at university.'

'Ah!'

From within the house Fiona Hobart's voice called, 'Is that somebody you're talking to Morgan, dear?'

'He's talking to his father.' Then, in a quieter tone as his wife entered the hall passage from the kitchen, 'More accurately, he's *not* talking to his father. At least he's not *saying* anything.'

'Come into the kitchen, dear.' Fiona held out a hand, as if to guide Hobart through his own house. 'I've just made a quick snack. Scrambled eggs. Morgan said he'd like some.'

'I'd love some scrambled eggs, but first of all I'd like to . . .'

'Good. Come through to the kitchen, dear.'

'I'd like to know why . . . ' Hobart realised, with some annoyance, that he was talking to his son's disappearing back and that his wife had already returned to the kitchen.

Hobart stood for a moment in order to take a firmer grasp upon his feelings. He was – and he knew this for an undoubted fact – a very moderate man. A man not given to flying off the handle. A patient man, with a tendency to think of other people's feelings before he either spoke or acted. If not a model husband, at least a husband who, within very wide limits, allowed his wife to dictate the pace and style of their marriage. If not a perfect father, at least one of those parents who genuinely *tried* to follow the strange meanderings of the modern mind.

In short, Hobart was a good and long-suffering man . . . and he'd have argued *that* point with anybody.

As he walked into the kitchen his movement was a little stiff-legged.

'There you are, dear.' Fiona Hobart placed a plate filled with scrambled eggs on the formica-topped kitchen table. 'I'll pop a couple of slices in the toaster.'

As she turned – as Hobart settled himself in the kitchen chair to enjoy the makeshift meal – he mentioned, as if in passing, 'I see Morgan's home.'

'Yes, dear.'

'Shouldn't he be at university?'

'Well – er . . .' She fed bread slices into the toaster and pressed the lever. 'Yes . . . he should.'

'Why isn't he?' asked Hobart, still in a pleasant and reasonable voice, as he loaded his fork.

'He's – er – he's come home, dear.' Fiona Hobart unhooked a beaker, placed it alongside the plate of scrambled eggs and poured freshly brewed tea. She repeated, 'He's come home.'

'Why?' Hobart raised the fork to his mouth.

'Dear?'

'Why has he come home? Is he ill?'

'Oh, no. He's quite well.'

'Has . . . ' Hobart chewed, then swallowed. ' . . . has the university burned down?'

'What?'

'The university. Has it been destroyed? Is *that* why he's come home?'

'Good Lord, no. Nothing like that.' Then, in a neat side-stepping movement, 'I heard the news about Lessford on the radio. Isn't it awful to think . . . '

'At the moment,' said Hobart, patiently, 'I am reserving all my thoughts for my son. Why is he at home?'

'It's – er – difficult.' She flapped her arms a little. 'I mean – y'know – it's not *easy*.'

'Fiona, my love.' Hobart raised a slightly quizzical eyebrow. He didn't know it, but his tone carried a depth of affection unusual for a man as many years married as

70

himself. 'Unlike our son, I did *not* enjoy the opportunity of a university education. But that does *not* imply that I'm a fool.' He paused, smiled and continued, 'Let me help you out, dear. Between us we've produced an idiot. An *educated* idiot. An idiot we wouldn't exchange for anybody else in the world. All that . . . but, an *idiot*. All I'm asking is that I be told of his latest idiocy.'

'Clarence, dear, I don't like you calling him a . . .'

'Please,' pleaded Hobart. 'Why has he come home?'

'They – they sent him home,' she said in a little-girl-lost voice.

'The university authorities?' He loaded the fork with scrambled eggs once more.

'Yes.' The toaster popped and she gave a tiny jump, then turned to remove the toast, as she repeated, 'Yes, dear. That's why he's here.'

'The university authorities sent him home?' mused Hobart. He chewed for a moment, then added, 'Does anybody know *why*?'

'Oh yes, dear. They've – y'know – dismissed him.'

'Expelled him?'

'Yes, dear,' she breathed.

She bent to the task of buttering toast and, for a moment, he seemed to concentrate all his attention upon eating scrambled eggs.

Then, he murmured, 'He must have done something. He didn't just become "redundant" – did he?'

'No. Not redundant.'

'Women?' asked Hobart, gently.

'No, dear. Not women. I think they . . .'

'Drunkenness?'

'Of course not. Morgan isn't the sort to . . .'

'Rowdyism? Hooliganism?'

'Certainly not.'

'He hasn't *stolen* anything, has he?'

'Clarence!'

'All right, dear.' He moved his empty fork in a slightly

71

hopeless gesture. 'Merely that I'm running out of options.'

'He – he says he was only experimenting,' she muttered.

'Experimenting? What with?'

She seemed to force the word 'drugs' from behind clenched teeth.

Hobart placed his knife and fork on the surface of the table at each side of his plate. It was a slow and deliberate movement. He still had his fingers around the handles of the knife and fork as he spoke. His voice was low and with the hint of a tremor.

'I would have preferred women. I would have preferred booze, or even theft.'

'Clarence!' She sensed the depth of hurt and it frightened her a little.

'Everything.' He slowly tilted his head and looked up at her. The near-defeat moistened his eyes and made his voice hoarse. 'Everything! Our child – my son . . . what *haven't* we given him?'

'We've done our best, dear,' she whispered.

'The book of words says it's our fault,' he muttered. 'Basically the parents' fault. That's what the experts say. He's lacked something. Some sort of emotional stability. Something we've denied him . . .'

'Darling, that's not *true*. That's not . . .'

' . . . something that's made him subconsciously rebel. Dammit, it's never *their* fault.' There was a terrible tautness in his words. 'It's never the fault of the addict. Never weakness. There's always some hidden reason. Something somebody *else* has done.' He took a deep and shuddering breath then, in a less tight but more bitter voice, said, 'We live in a crazy world, my dear. A *crazy* world. The values – *our* values – have been stood on their head. People like me – coppers – we're "the enemy" these days. We stop "fun". We prevent "freedom". Ask him.' He jerked his head. 'Ask him upstairs. Ask our son. Ask him to be honest, and tell you what he and his modern friends think of policemen.'

And still they talked, and both Gilliant and Harris wondered just why McQuilly and Roper had raced north from the fastness of the Met. To do with the helicopter crash . . . it was far too coincidental to be other than that. To do with drug abuse . . . that, too, otherwise both McQuilly and Roper wouldn't have concentrated so much of the conversation upon the subject.

But where the hell the two subjects met was still a mystery.

Harris pointedly folded back the left cuff of his jacket and glanced at his watch. McQuilly, equally pointedly, ignored the gesture and continued speaking.

' . . . the Islamic Jihad extremists and the various groups under Arafat seem to have taken to the drug weapon without much difficulty. In Italy the Red Brigade appear to be ready to use whatever means they can get hold of in a prolonged attempt to undermine democratic society. Heroin and cocaine. Safer than bombs and more certain than bullets. The terrorists are starting to realise the truth of that.'

'Dope? Terrorists?' Harris muttered the two questions in an exploratory tone.

'That's why we're here, assistant chief constable,' confirmed Roper.

'The IRA?' Gilliant added his question to those of Harris.

'That, too, is why we're here,' agreed McQuilly. 'To date the Provisional IRA have refused to touch drugs. They claim moral grounds. Actually, it's to keep the support of a lot of people who *wouldn't* support them if they *used* the drug weapon. We'd like to keep it that way.'

They walked along the pavement and were unhappy. They clasped hands as they walked because they were still very much in love and because the love they had for each other seemed to reflect and magnify their misery. Ralph and Helen had had the same love for each other, but now Helen was dead. The unexpected proof of their own mortality made them cling more firmly to each other.

'I think it might break him,' breathed Alva.

Hoyle nodded.

'Will he . . . ' She closed her mouth.

'What?'

'Do anything silly,' she whispered. 'Y'know – silly. You don't think he *will*, do you?'

'Commit suicide?' said Hoyle, flatly.

'*Might* he?'

'It's possible. I think *I* would.'

'Don't! Please *don't*.' But what it was she was urging wasn't clear. Perhaps not to voice her own fears. Perhaps not even to think of them.

It was late afternoon. The home-goers were not yet on the streets. The shops were not yet closed and the offices were not yet empty. The seekers after entertainment were not yet in sufficient numbers to make any appreciable difference. It was a time of day when Lessford, like every other city, seemed to pause for breath. It was a morose, hollow, haunting time and the mood of the city matched the mood of David and Alva Hoyle.

'I should have stayed with him,' murmured Alva, sadly.

'No.'

'I *should*.' There was passionate self-guilt in the last word.

'No,' repeated Hoyle.

'I know. He insisted. But, at a time like this a man needs somebody to . . . '

'We did what he asked.'

'I know. But . . .'

'We telephoned his brother.'

'That's not enough, David.'

'It's all he asked.'

'I feel rotten,' she muttered. 'We should have stayed . . . one of us.'

'No.' His voice was low and brittle and he seemed to bite the word off.

'Look, if he's . . .'

'He needs space.'

'What?'

'Space. Elbow room.'

'Space?'

'In which to weep.'

'Oh!'

'Alone. Privately.'

'You – you think he'll . . .'

'Of course he will.' And now his tone seemed laced with suppressed anger.

'In that case we should have . . .'

'Alva, he's a copper. A chief superintendent, for God's sake. He has his pride.'

'Pride? What on earth has pride . . .'

'Men,' interrupted Hoyle, heavily. And all the anger had gone. Only a sad honesty remained. 'Men have different priorities. *Wrong* priorities, maybe. But, coppers. High-ranking coppers in particular.' They'd reached the car-park and as he unlocked the door of the car Hoyle continued speaking in a low voice, but without looking at his wife. 'He'll weep. Of course he'll weep. We know that. He *knows* we know he'll weep. But there's a pretence. An important pretence. There's an act to be gone through.' He opened the door and, as she climbed into the front passenger seat, he continued, 'God willing, he'll come through it. He'll come back to work. Normality – that'll be another pretence. That, and the job he holds. The rank he carries. A detective chief superintendent weak enough to be heartbroken? Weak enough to cry? Not strong enough – not tough enough – to hold back the tears when people are around – even friends? That's for the future. But there's a part of him that's already trying to *see* that future. How rough it might be. How near-impossible. How *utterly* impossible if he's ever tagged by those who don't know him as a "weak man". Give him space, my pet. Give him privacy. At the moment, that's all he wants.'

32

Sergeant Reeve entered the ante-room of the mortuary at a speed slightly in excess of his usual walking pace. Reeve wondered what the hell was going on. He had grave doubts about whether anybody *knew* what was going on. Anybody! First of all a runaway horse in the small hours of the morning, then a full-blooded murder enquiry, then a crashed helicopter followed by a swift melting away of all the coppers necessary to run that enquiry and now an urgent radio message for him to get to the morgue at Lessford Hospital on wide throttle. The Keystone Cops were top class intel-ligentsia by comparison.

'Is he in there?' Reeve didn't even break his stride as he snapped the question at the mortuary attendant.

'Eh?' The sudden intrusion of this excess of life in this place reserved for death made the mortuary attendant jump.

'The saw-bones? The scalpel wallah?'

'The pathologist?'

'Is he *in* there?' demanded Reeve.

'Yes. I think he's performing an autopsy on . . .'

But Reeve was past the swing-doors and out of earshot.

The pathologist was dressed for business; heavy rubber apron over green, ankle-length overall; rubber boots and rubber gloves. The autopsy table held a cadaver and, around the edge of the table, knives, saws and nippers were ready to hand. He looked up as Reeve entered.

'I was told to come here,' announced Reeve.

'Really? Who by?' The pathologist looked surprised.

'By radio. I was out on The Tops and I got a message to come here. They sent it out via one of the squad cars.'

'Who sent it out?' The pathologist still looked surprised.

'From the radio room. From *here* . . . Lessford. That I'd to get myself to the mortuary, tout suite, because the pathologist wanted to see me.'

'*I* wanted to see *you*?' The pathologist looked even more puzzled.

'Presumably about the murder,' explained Reeve, heavily.

'Ah, the murder of the girl on The Tops?' Light dawned.

'I take it that's what . . . '

'But I asked for Chief Superintendent Flensing.'

'Nobody said anything about Flensing.'

'Or, if not Flensing, Detective Chief Inspector Hoyle.'

'Nor anything about Hoyle. Just me. That *I* had to contact you as soon as possible.'

'Good God, man! *You're* not in charge of a murder enquiry.' It was not meant to be a snub. The pathologist was a decent enough man. He'd worked with coppers too many times not to know that theirs, too, could be a thankless job. But he was human and, much as his work fascinated him, he'd been presented with far too many stiffs for one day. Therefore his irritation showed and the words *sounded* like a snub.

Reeve scowled his displeasure, then asked, 'Is it something you've found during the post mortem?'

'What?'

'Something you think the police should know?'

'Well – yes – it is . . . actually.'

'*I'm* "the police",' said Reeve in a flat, uncompromising tone.

'You're only a . . . '

'I represent the *police*, doctor,' interrupted Reeve. 'You may not like what I'm wearing on my sleeves but, for the moment, that's all you're *getting*.'

'Oh!'

'I'm up to the eyeballs in the murder thing. Everybody else seems to be galloping around picking up pieces of helicopter so, if you've anything to say, *say* it.'

'Look, sergeant, I don't mean to imply that you're not . . .'

'The hell you don't!'

'All right!' The pathologist held up his gloved hands in token surrender. 'I'll tell *you*. Why not? When you next see either Mr Flensing or Mr Hoyle you can pass the information on.'

33

It must be confessed that the Parker household represented the earache of matrimonial harmony. The fights were continuous and varied; they ranged from slanging matches and sulks, to walk-outs and, occasionally, the hurling of crockery; their subject-matter covered television programmes, housework, parenthood, in-laws, gardening, interior and exterior decorating and, of course, money. Nor were the alliances ever other than shifting. With two sons and two daughters, all of whom gave an outward appearance of unqualified detestation of the other three, it was anybody's guess which side of the war they would each support.

'Horse shit!' Parker was complaining. 'I had to go all the way to the laboratory with two parcels of horse . . .'

'Father!' The elder daughter closed her eyes in disgust. She was an ambitious young lady eager to attract the attention of the junior partner in the firm of accountants where she worked as a telephonist. Secretly she wished she'd have had a better chance by being born into a more select family. She compressed her lips and said, 'We don't need the sordid details.'

'Not when we're eating,' added her mother.

'You're eating potatoes,' Parker reminded them.

'I don't see what . . .'

'That's what they were grown in.'

'Oh, my God!' The elder daughter lowered her fork.

'Your father,' said Mrs Parker, 'is a cretin, with a cretinous sense of humour.'

'Good spuds, though.' This grinning observation came from the younger son.

'You wouldn't know,' sneered the younger daughter. 'With all that butter you won't be able to taste the potato.'

'Butter is very bad for you,' pronounced the elder daughter.

'Hey!' Parker waggled his fork, threateningly. 'This is a meal, not the Houses of bloody Parliament. Less talking and more chewing . . . right?'

'How does *she* know it's bad for you?' demanded the younger son.

'By the way.' Parker glanced round the table for a quick head-count before committing himself. 'Where's Wally?'

'Band practice.' Mrs Parker answered the question without breaking the rhythm of her jaw. 'Can't you *ever* remember?'

'I'm not musical.'

'Wally isn't, either,' quipped the younger daughter. 'The row he makes on that tenor horn. It's enough to . . .'

'He can play *Poet and Peasant*,' said Mrs Parker. '*And* without too many mistakes.'

The elder daughter looked suitably disgusted, and said, 'Mother, that's not *music*.'

'I like it.'

'What is it, then?' The younger son came to the rescue of his brother. 'If *Poet and Peasant* isn't music, what is? That's what I'd like to know.'

'I'm talking about opera.' The elder daughter tipped her nose slightly. 'Symphony. The classics.'

'*Poet and Peasant*'s a classic. It's an opera.'

79

'It's an *overture*. A very *ordinary* overture.'

'It's an overture to an opera.'

'Every overture isn't an overture to . . .'

'Hell's bells!' exploded Parker. 'I've been up all night. I've walked bloody miles across those moors, collecting horse shit. I come back home for a bit of peace and a bite to eat and, all of a sudden, I'm in the middle of a daft argument about music. If Wally can play *Poet and Peasant* good luck to him. Just don't let him practise around here, when I've finished this meal and gone to bed.'

The remark was, of course, tempting fate and in order to prove that fate claimed the last laugh the telephone began to ring as Parker stopped talking. Reeve was rounding up as many buckshee coppers as possible because Reeve was suddenly the officer responsible for keeping a murder enquiry rolling.

34

'We have a man well placed.' McQuilly seemed to find some difficulty in finding the right words. The soft drawl carried as much quiet authority as ever, nevertheless the slight hesitation suggested a certain embarrassment. He added, 'It's taken us years to get him there.'

'To get him fully accepted,' added Roper.

'Sergeant Roper,' explained McQuilly, 'is something of an expert on IRA matters. The structure. The tactics. The powers behind the throne. That sort of thing.'

Harris moved his eyes from McQuilly to Roper, then back to McQuilly.

'Not the sort of specialisation we go in for up here,' murmured Gilliant.

'Quite.'

'Cloak and dagger stuff,' grunted Harris.

'Of necessity, Mr Harris.'

'Buggering about playing real-life James Bond.'

'Not like that at all, assistant chief constable.' Roper's eyes glinted. 'Those people use real bullets. And they don't *explain* what they're going to do. They demonstrate, before you can duck.'

'Sergeant.' McQuilly quietened the spat of anger being shown by his companion. Still choosing his words, he continued, 'The man we're talking about – "our" man – has some influence with the Provisionals. He's up there among the policy-makers. He has influence.'

'Agent provocateur,' growled Harris. 'Super-grass. All that sort of garbage.'

'Harris!' This time Gilliant slammed on the brakes. Hard.

Harris tightened his jaw, made to move from his chair, and muttered, 'If I'm not required . . .'

'You're required,' snapped Gilliant.

'If I can't express an opinion . . .'

'You can also express an opinion. What you *can't* do is hawk your bias around.'

'Assistant chief constable.' McQuilly moved in to steady the rocking boat. 'Have you ever *seen* a man knee-capped? Have you ever heard him scream?'

Harris breathed hard, but didn't answer.

'I have,' said McQuilly. 'So has Sergeant Roper. It isn't an experience you forget. And, if the identity of the man you seem determined to scorn ever becomes known, knee-capping will merely be the hors-d'oeuvre to a positive banquet of pain. These men are fanatics, Mr Harris. They're not "criminals" in the normal sense of the word. We call them "terrorists", but they believe themselves to be "freedom fighters". Their numbers have never reached the five-hundred mark but, because of the way they operate, they require a small army of highly trained soldiers merely to contain them. Without that containment Ireland – north and south – would become a bloodbath.

'We *can* contain them. But, only if we know what they're

up to. Only if we know their next move, before they make it. It calls for strange policing, Mr Harris.' The smile was fresh from the deep freeze. '*Dangerous policing*. The RUC, the UDR and even the SAS send undercover men in, with the expectation that they'll be identified. To a limited extent they are the smoke-screen. Occasionally – very occasionally – *we* feed the information to the enemy via which they're caught.'

Harris muttered, 'Of all the filthy, double-crossing . . . '

'Not quite "James Bond".' McQuilly's tone was softly mocking. 'Too evil for clean-cut spies who prefer their vodka stirred to shaken. But that's what we deal in, assistant chief constable. Evil! Our evil and their evil. Our job is to assess the various evils and make sure we end up with the *least* evil – in the long term.'

'That's not *my* . . . '

'Ah, but it *is*.' McQuilly's interruption was accompanied by slightly raised eyebrows. 'It's why we're here. To make sure it *is* your job.'

'You can't make me . . . '

'We *can*!'

McQuilly glanced at Gilliant.

Gilliant gave a single, slow nod then, in an expressionless tone, said, 'They *can*, Mr Harris. It isn't often they *do*. But they *can*.'

'How the hell . . . '

'When you've a moment to spare,' said McQuilly, 'it might interest you to glance through your chief constable's Person File. For a period of his service he was one of us.'

'Oh!'

'Fortunately.' Again the cold smile came and went. 'It saves us time. We don't have to draw diagrams.'

'Accept it, Harris,' sighed Gilliant.

Harris remained silent and stone-faced.

'Our priority,' drawled McQuilly, 'is to keep the drug weapon out of the area. Or if we can't keep it out, to know

82

when and where to expect it. Arms caches are unimportant by comparison. The man we have in there – the man who's part of the IRA council – *must* be protected. He exerts influence. He keeps us informed. It's taken us years to get him there and he must be *kept* there.'

35

It was not the end of the world. Flensing would have argued the point, but it was *not* the end of the world. Merely (or so it seemed) the end of *his* world.

Ralph Flensing – the detective chief superintendent whose reputation was firmly based upon an ability to ride the rough and the smooth with equal ease – and he was like an over-imaginative child abandoned in a House of Horrors. The grief bordered upon mindless panic. He sat motionless in a chair – not even a comfortable chair, but an upright wooden-seated chair in the kitchen of his home – and stared at the tiled wall beyond the fridge. A fridge *she* had never seen, a wall *she* had never seen in a house *she* had never entered.

He daren't move.

To move would mean he'd have to do what had to be done, and one of the first things that had to be done was to visit the hospital. To see her. To *look* at her. To acknowledge that she was, indeed, dead.

His racing mind skidded away from the subject. It was something beyond his present contemplation.

Never mind what David and Alva Hoyle had said. Never mind their obvious sincerity. Whilever *he* didn't see her body there remained the hair-line-thin possibility that there'd been a mistake. The miracle was still there. A mistake – and Helen was still alive.

Indeed, she *was* still alive. She had to be. His brain was, for the moment, past his control and his brain insisted that

Helen was still *alive*. Fastened within the confines of that blasted iron lung, but still alive and waiting to turn her head and smile a greeting when next he opened the door of the side ward.

Thus the boiling, brazen turmoil of his thoughts. The madness which raged under the dome of his skull. And he daren't move, or shift the steadiness of his gaze. To do so would have snapped the gossamer skin of self-deception and reality would have rushed in and drowned him.

36

'Am I under arrest?' Cossitter demanded.

'No, sir.'

'Not "helping the police in their enquiries"? Nothing like that?'

'No, sir,' sighed the DC. 'Nothing like that.'

The detective constable was stranded up the proverbial gum tree. Since putting his uniform in mothballs less than two years ago – since he began wearing that other 'uniform', the loose-fitting mac and the sports jacket – his forte had been petty crooks. Petty crooks and mildly obnoxious perverts. Handbag snatchers, creeps who'd pocketed bits and pieces from the open stalls of multiple stores and, of course, finks who figured their genitalia was worth a passing glance by respectable ladies walking along and minding their own business. What the old hands called 'thick-ear policing'. Nick 'em, bounce 'em along to the nearest cell then leave 'em to simmer in their own juice till they were ready to cough. The simple arithmetic of law-enforcement, with no frills.

And now he was into the higher mathematics of a murder enquiry and Detective Constable Dobson was no forensic Einstein.

'I think we should wait,' he said, hopefully.

'Wait?'

'For Detective Inspector Hobart.'

'*You* wait,' barked Cossitter. 'I'm going to *do* something.'

'Sir, you can't . . .'

'Can't what? What is it I *can't* do? Good God, man, it's my daughter who's been stabbed to death. It's my . . .'

'We don't know that yet, sir.'

'All right, take me into Lessford, or wherever the corpse is, and let me make an identification. I'm blasted *sure*, but if you still entertain any doubts . . .'

'I rather think it *is* your daughter, sir,' said Dobson, sadly.

'So, what the hell are we waiting for?'

Dobson couldn't answer. The truth was, Dobson himself didn't know what they were waiting for. Indeed, Dobson was rapidly reaching a frightening conclusion: that the whole murder enquiry had somehow come unstitched and that *he* had been left holding a particularly messy baby. Why else would Hobart have absented himself for so long? Why else wasn't Hoyle, or even Flensing, ranting and raging in the near-vicinity.

'Where . . .' Dobson swallowed. ' . . . where do you want to go, sir?'

'Apple Tree Farm. Where else?'

Cossitter hauled himself from the armchair. It was an awkward, cumbersome movement in which the arms of the chair took a lot of strain. It meant pulling, then pushing, until the artificial legs were upright and Cossitter's body was perched on top of them. It caused Dobson slight embarrassment to watch and he wondered whether he should step forward to help, but had second thoughts. This barking, Yorkshire-terrier of a man was something new in Dobson's experience. Not too long ago, he'd wept. Then, as suddenly as they'd started, the tears had stopped and it was as if they'd never been. The gleam of perpetual anger was back in his eyes and, despite the consumption of whisky, there was no sign of drunkenness.

Cossitter snapped, 'The Perkins tart might know something.'

'Who?'

'Perkins. Mary Perkins. She was at school with my daughter. One of those stupid "best friend" relationships.'

'Oh!'

'Didn't you *know*?'

'Well – no . . . I . . . '

'God Almighty!' Cossitter's nostrils quivered.

'No doubt Inspector Hobart knew,' said Dobson, hurriedly.

'*Knew!* Has the damn man lost interest? Isn't he on the case any more? Has he taken off for some other . . . '

'Knows,' interrupted Dobson, and his tone bordered upon desperation. '*Knows*. When he gets back he'll . . . '

'He'll find me missing.'

'Oh!'

'Laddie, I have no intention of sitting here, sucking my thumb, while your blasted inspector hides away in a corner, somewhere, contemplating his navel.'

'I'll – I'll come with you, sir,' gulped Dobson. Then, almost apologetically, 'If you don't mind.'

'Why not?' snapped Cossitter. 'You might as well make yourself useful, and drive.'

37

It was one of those summer evenings oldsters talk about but never expect to see again. It had been a sizzling day, with the promise of a hot and airless night, but the evening seemed to give a few hours of respite; the sun had lost its full blaze and the imagination conjured up the first stirrings of a breeze.

The house had a walled garden at the rear. It had a fair-sized lawn with fair-sized flower beds and a fair-sized greenhouse. Above all it had privacy, and David Hoyle sought that privacy as he fought the misery which threatened to choke him.

Even his wife Alva, whom he loved dearly and counted as the most precious person alive, couldn't comfort him and she was wise enough to recognise the truth and allow him to prowl the short-cropped lawn alone.

Detective Chief Superintendent Ralph Flensing was far more than a respected senior officer. Far more than a fellow-copper and colleague. Even far more than a friend.

Few people would have understood because it happens only rarely. Coppers tend towards individualism and, because of the nature of their job, they also tend to be suspicious. They are even suspicious of each other. The reason is simple. They encounter liars whose lies have the ring of truth and whose lies prevent the natural progression of basic justice. They listen to excuses and reasons *for* excuses until the point is reached when every excuse is brushed aside as one more empty reason for contemptuous conduct. They see good men smashed and evil men applauded until, eventually, they build a hard shell of mistrust around themselves and allow only a very limited number of people to penetrate that shell. And rarely indeed is one of those people a fellow-policeman.

Yet it can happen and it had happened between Hoyle and Flensing.

Equally, albeit not as strangely, it had happened between Alva Hoyle and Helen Flensing.

Thereafter, the quartet had fused into a perfectly balanced grouping, with the immaculate symmetry of the petals which go to make a flawless flower. And now one of the petals was missing and the flower was ruined.

His utter helplessness amplified Hoyle's misery. He was a copper, and coppers *did* things. When life fell out of plumb they didn't sit around like so many ninnies. They knew how to get things back to normal. Knew who to telephone. Who to contact. They could pull strings and get things righted. They could play hell, if necessary. They could twist a few arms, stamp on a few corns and bloody a few noses. Damnation, coppers could *do* something.

But not this time.

And yet, he had truly loved Helen Flensing. Admittedly, it

had been a strange love, but had been no less pure for that. It had not been a carnal love, nor yet the familial love of a brother for a sister. It had been something different and something very special. It had started with the unqualified admiration for a woman encased in an iron lung who, via some magic, retained a glowing femininity. And always a very pristine admiration, unsullied by even a hint of sympathy.

Helen. Helen who had been so alive. So much more alive than most women, despite her inability to breathe without mechanical aid. Helen who, at the beginning, he'd admired but who, because of what she was, had commanded far more than admiration.

Thereafter had come this feeling of closeness. The laughter. The warmth when they'd all four been together and that damned metal contraption had been forgotten.

Ralph and Helen, Alva and himself.

More than friendship and far more than understanding.

Love!

There had been four of them. Now there were only three. One day there'd be only two. Then only one.

He stopped his pacing and hurried into the house. His wife was waiting and, as he held her in his arms, she felt the moisture on his cheeks and understood.

38

'We meet again,' said Reeve, sardonically.

Parker sniffed his disgust.

'I didn't interrupt anything, I trust.'

'I was having a meal,' grunted Parker.

'Hard lines. Bang goes your digestive juices.'

'I was thinking about going to bed.'

'Coppers aren't supposed to sleep during murder enquiries. Cat-naps, fags and cups of char. That's what keeps 'em going – so I'm told.'

'Sergeant,' snarled Parker, 'I don't take a big enough pay cheque home to merit being arsed around like this. I'm paid to obey orders . . . '

'It's nice to know you realise *that*.'

' . . . not to walk bloody miles looking for horse droppings. I have a home. I have a family . . . '

'That's something of a novelty.'

' . . . who like to have me around.'

'Don't bet money on it.'

It was quite a cross-talk act while it lasted. Two aggrieved men, both of whom should have been happily taking orders while other men accepted responsibilities. They shared the front seats of Reeve's motor car and stared at a spot where, some few hours before, they'd found the body of a murdered woman.

'Where *is* everybody?' complained Parker.

'Don't think I haven't asked.'

'Well – all right – where *are* they?'

'That helicopter thing.'

'For Christ's sake! Not *everybody*.'

'This,' said Reeve, heavily, 'is where it all started. This and a horse.'

'Sergeant, if you seriously think I'm going to . . . '

'And she was strangled. Not stabbed.'

'Eh?' Parker's jaw dropped a little.

'That's what the saw-bones says. The knife went in *after* she was dead. That's why there wasn't much blood. The hyoid bone's snapped. That means she was strangled.'

'In that case, why the hell . . . '

'Don't ask questions, Parker.' Reeve blew out his cheeks. 'Don't ask *me* questions. Come up with somebody we *can* throw a few questions at, then we'll get cracking.'

'Hey, what's all this plural pronoun stuff?' Parker looked startled. 'Don't get too heavy on the "we" bit. I'm only a common-or-garden . . . '

'Wouldn't you *like* to detect a murder?' interrupted Reeve.

'I don't give a damn.' Parker was worried enough to be honest. 'Some silly cow gets herself strangled. It won't put *me* off my grub.'

'It's your beat,' Reeve reminded him.

'Okay. I work it. I keep it tidy.'

'Except for the odd corpse, here and there.'

'Coppers,' explained Parker in a world-weary tone. 'Coppers – ordinary, run-of-the-mill coppers – ordinary, run-of-the-mill sergeants – do *not* detect murder. People like us brew the tea and fetch the fags. Reeve, the "Sergeant Cluffs" of this world don't exist. They're like unicorns. They're not around except in the imagination of blokes who write books. They're not *real*.'

'It *has* been done.' Reeve didn't sound too sure, and qualified the remark with, 'It *must* have been done.'

'Where? When?'

'It *must* have been,' repeated Reeve.

'You're kidding yourself,' mocked Parker.

'All right, it's going to *be* done.' Reeve's patience was wearing thin. 'Christ only knows where the flash boys are, but this is your patch and my responsibility and I, for one, want to get back to a quiet life. I don't like silly buggers killing people on *my* doorstep. So, I'm going to do something about it.'

'You?' sneered Parker.

'With your help.'

'Look, if you think . . . '

'I *know*!' Without being aware of it, Reeve thrust his chin a fraction of an inch forward. In a hard, no-nonsense voice he continued, 'We know her name. Anthea Cossitter. The pathologist slipped that one out. And you, Constable Parker, are going to scour what few brains you have in that skull of yours until you come up with a few more names. Locals who might know her. Snitches . . . assuming you have such things on this God-forsaken beat. I don't give a damn if we're at it till you've grown that full set of whiskers you're so keen on.

Believe me, lad, *this* time you're going to do a bloody sight more than brew the tea and fetch the fags.'

39

The forensic science laboratory liaison officer hummed and hawed a little. His was an invidious position. He was a police inspector but the rank carried only the pay; he had little authority and even less responsibility; he was neither uniformed nor CID. He was the official conduit between the police and the scientists, was neither one nor the other and took orders from both.

At first it had seemed one of the proverbial 'cushy numbers'. Office hours, a neat little office near the entrance of the laboratory building, the easy companionship of men and women learned in the various sciences harnessed to the detection of crime and a certain standing within the community of his fellow-officers.

His main duties demanded that he know the various forms which require to be completed before specimens and exhibits were allowed to be examined. To know which department of the laboratory each specimen or exhibit should be forwarded to. To give some approximation of the time required for a scientific examination. To officially notify the result of that examination to the appropriate officer.

He was a man of rote. He would argue (and often *did* argue) that, in a building staffed by experts who tended towards the eccentric or the absent-mindedness of the specialist, his was the firm hand of order. He it was who ensured that order did not give way to chaos.

Unfortunately he was no decision-maker. If 'B' did not follow 'A' and immediately precede 'C' the forensic science laboratory liaison officer was well out of his depth.

He said, 'Well, I don't know about that,' and the man who had just presented his credentials knew he was bluffing.

'You know now,' smiled the man.

'Yes, but . . .'

'Get your boffins away from the scene.'

'I – er – I don't know whether I have the authority.'

'I've just *given* you the authority.' The man continued to smile, but the smile became slightly fixed and without friendship.

The liaison officer said, 'I'd have thought the Civil Aviation people.'

'No. The Home Office.'

'It's just that . . .'

'You have the authority.' The man tapped the letter he'd handed to the liaison officer. 'That's all you need. Any arguments, ring London and they'll verify. Meanwhile, get your forensic people away from the crash and my men will take over.'

'The director . . .' began the liaison officer.

'Like you.' There was no mistaking the warning. 'The director of the laboratory will do what he's told – or stand the consequences.'

'I'll – I'll tell him.'

'*Instruct* him,' corrected the man.

40

For the moment Clarence Hobart was no longer a detective inspector. He wasn't even a police officer. He was a husband and a father, and that's *all* he was. Murder and mayhem beyond the walls of this, his own private little world, concerned him not at all. Women could have knives driven into their bodies, horses could run wild across moorland, detective chief superintendents could do cartwheels, even Harris could dive, feet first, into the nearest lake. Nothing – but *nothing* – had priority over the task in hand.

And yet . . .

Things had to be said, but he didn't know how to say them.

He was in his son's bedroom-cum-den and his son, Morgan, was sitting on the divan bed waiting. Morgan had a slightly worried expression on his face. Not too worried – past experience insisted that he could twist his mother around his little finger and she, in turn, could make the old man run up any wall she fancied – therefore he wasn't *too* worried. Moreover, they were playing on his (Morgan's) home ground. This room was *his*. The hi-fi equipment, the computer-cum-word-processor, the TV set, the wall posters, the 'Please Adjust Your Dress Before Leaving' sign on the closed door. These, and a score of other things, tended to make the old man uncomfortable. His was a china-ducks-on-the-wall mentality – a never-swear-in-mixed-company way of life – therefore (to take an example) the art reproduction above the bed showing a nude in a classic pornographic pose caused embarrassment enough to make sure the old man never actually *looked* at it.

A little worry, therefore, but not too much. Without doubt the old lady had softened him up. He'd be a comparative pushover.

Hobart leaned his back against the closed door, shoved his hands into the pockets of his trousers and, for a few moments, eyed his son with complete non-understanding.

At last, and in a remarkably calm and controlled voice, Hobart said, 'Your mother tells me you've left university.'

'Yeah.' Morgan nodded. He settled himself more comfortably on the divan bed.

'That the authorities *asked* you to leave.'

'Something like that.'

'That they *made* you leave.'

'Yeah.' Another nod.

'Forgive me.' Hobart's voice was calm and reasonable. 'I like to get the terminology right. You've been *expelled*?'

'That's what it boils down to.'

'Specifically,' insisted Hobart. 'Not "what it boils down

93

to". If I don't understand, I'll tell you.'

'Yeah. Expelled.'

'Not merely suspended?'

'No.' Morgan's worry went a notch higher. The old man was deliberately making things as rough as possible. He said, 'Not suspended. Expelled.'

'You must have done something,' murmured Hobart.

'Yeah.'

'What?'

'I – er – y'know – experimented a little.'

'Experimented?' Hobart's eyebrows lifted, enquiringly.

'With dope,' said Morgan, flatly.

'Again, can we be specific?'

'Look, pop . . .'

'Specifically,' insisted Hobart.

'Aw – y'know . . . ' Morgan moved his hands in a meaningless gesture.

'When you tell me, then I'll know.'

'Skag,' muttered Morgan.

'Heroin. Is that all?'

'Coke. I've sniffed coke a couple of times. No more.'

'Heroin and cocaine. Anything else?'

'No.' Morgan shook his head.

'Cannabis?'

'No.'

'Amphetamines?'

'No.'

'LSD?'

'No. For Christ's sake, I've told you. Skag and coke, that's all. Everybody takes *them*.'

'Everybody?'

'Look, pop . . .'

'How many other expulsions?'

'Eh?'

'If, as you say, everybody takes heroin and cocaine, how many other people have been expelled from the university?'

'Just me,' mumbled Morgan. 'I was unlucky.'

Hobart moistened his lips, then asked, 'Are you an addict? And I want the truth.'

'No. Of course not.'

'None of them ever are,' observed Hobart, bitterly.

'Look, I swear to God . . . '

'Why you?' demanded Hobart. 'If "everybody" indulges – if you're not yet addicted – why Morgan Hobart?'

'A clampdown.' There was even a touch of outrage in his tone. 'The pigs wanted to make a name for themselves, so . . . '

He closed his mouth in mid-sentence.

'Have you been charged?' asked Hobart, gently.

'No. Just reported to the authorities.'

'Therefore, the "pigs" didn't want to make *much* of a name for themselves.'

'Look, pop, I don't mean to . . . '

'Do you still smoke?' interrupted Hobart. 'I don't mean pot. Ordinary cigarettes. Do you still smoke them?'

'Yeah. Why?'

'If you have one to spare, please?' Hobart removed a hand from its pocket.

Morgan looked startled, and said, 'I didn't know you . . . '

'So many things.' Hobart held out a hand. 'So *very* many things about me you don't know.'

There was a silence while Morgan took cigarettes and matches from the drawer of a bedside locker. Until Hobart had lighted one of the cigarettes and enjoyed the first couple of deep inhalations. It was not a temporary truce because, as yet, there had't been a war. And yet something was *being* said – something was *going* to be said – and the subtleties of his father's conversation worried Morgan. The nuances, the emphases and, most of all, the calm certainty. Like ice, but very thin ice and, if it broke, somebody would be dumped in sub-zero water to drown. It was scary. It wasn't *like* his father.

'I didn't always have a gut,' observed Hobart, mildly.

'Eh?' Morgan stared.

'Blame your mother's cooking for that. I was once fit and slim. In the old days – when I was new in the force – I'd quite a name. I could handle myself.'

'Look, pop, I don't know what . . .'

'I could take somebody like you and, without much of an effort, break a few bones.' He raised the cigarette to his lips, then, as he expelled the smoke, added 'I think I still could. It's a knack. I think I still have it.'

Morgan waited. What was being said – what was being implied – really *was* scary and, quite suddenly, Morgan realised why this father of his had made the rank of detective inspector.

Still in the same quiet, conversational tone, Hobart continued, 'I'm really two men, you see. I'm what your mother wants me to be – that on the outside and most of the time – but I'm also what I was before we met . . . your mother, I mean. Not a very nice sort of person. Do you follow?'

'Well – no – I don't . . .'

'Stand up.' And, when Morgan pushed himself from the bed, Hobart moved his head and added, 'Step a little closer.'

Morgan took a couple of steps towards his father. Hobart raised the cigarette to his lips, then removed it with his left hand. At the same time, he brought his right hand up and across in a back-handed blow that was still gathering speed when it landed on Morgan's mouth. It lifted the younger man from his feet and catapulted him back on to the bed.

'That's what I mean,' murmured Hobart.

Morgan gasped as he wiped the blood which was already trickling from his lips. He stared at his father. At the cigarette, whose ash hadn't even been disturbed.

'We're not supposed to do that,' said Hobart, sadly. 'All the experts agree. When your child turns into a junkie you're supposed to show him love and affection. Not smack his ears off.' He paused to draw on the cigarette. In the same, easy-going tone, he continued, 'That's okay. You're not a child. You're a man. You put away childish things years ago. The dolls you *now* play with play back.'

'Pop, I'm . . . ' Morgan dabbed at his bleeding mouth with a handkerchief. 'Let me say . . . '

'No,' interrupted Hobart, gently, 'let *me* say. I claim the privilege of age. Let me talk about my wife.'

'Ma? What's . . . '

'My wife,' repeated Hobart. 'She's important. To me, she's very important. I love her.' Then, before Morgan could say what he was about to say, 'Now "love" . . . there's a word you know a lot about. But not, necessarily, the emotion *I* have in mind. Your "love" requires the removal of panties. What I'm talking about doesn't. But what it *does* mean is this. If any man – *any* man – hurts my wife, insults my wife, offends my wife or causes my wife unnecessary worry he becomes my enemy. I don't just dislike him. I *hate* him and have the urge to hurt him . . . badly.'

'Look, pop – I'm sorry.'

'Sorry?' There was gentle mockery in the question.

'Yeah – y'know . . . *sorry*.'

'No.' Hobart shook his head. 'You're not sorry. You're *scared*. This fat-gutted guy you once took for granted isn't the mug you thought he was. There's a certain area of his life that's very dangerous. His wife. Upset his wife too much and, who the hell you are, you have *reason* to be scared.'

'Okay.' Morgan held his hand to his mouth and spoke through the handkerchief. There was a slight tremble in his voice, as he continued, 'Okay, you're right. I'm scared.'

'Good. You have *some* sense.'

'I'm – I'm also sorry. Very sorry.'

'The rules.' Hobart drew on the cigarette. 'Simple rules, but very strict rules. Forget "higher education". That's money down the drain. You find a job. I don't give a damn what it is. Bar-tender, sweeper-up . . . anything. We start

97

with the proposition that you're thick. Unskilled. Forget the unemployment statistics. You start walking, you start knocking on doors, you get a job. One month from today you start bringing home a wage. Two-thirds of that wage goes to your mother. You buy your own clothes from the remaining one-third. Holidays you pay for out of your own pocket. You're with me so far . . . are you?'

Morgan nodded.

'Good.' Hobart raised the cigarette to his mouth for the last time. He strolled across the room and squashed what remained of the cigarette into an ash-tray as he concluded, 'No dope of any kind. If I even *suspect* you of it you're out. No argument. No pleading. No excuse. Out! With a damn good thrashing to take with you. No excessive booze. No birds. And we'll start by ripping filthy pictures from these walls. Those are the rules. Take them, or leave them – and, to be honest, I don't give a spit-in-the-wind which choice you make.'

41

Gilliant replaced the receiver. His expression carried a genuine mix of concern and sadness.

'My Head of CID,' he said.

'Flensing?' Harris looked puzzled.

Still speaking to McQuilly, Gilliant continued, 'Bad news. His wife died suddenly, today. To let me know he won't be in until after the funeral.'

'I'm sorry,' murmured McQuilly.

'There's the murder enquiry,' growled Harris.

Gilliant nodded.

'Murder?' This time McQuilly looked puzzled.

'Out on one of the more isolated parts of the police district,' explained Gilliant. 'A young woman was murdered, last night. Flensing was co-ordinating the enquiries.'

'Oh!'

'Now what?' demanded Harris.

'Chief Inspector Hoyle can take over.' Gilliant sounded confident.

'Can he?' Harris did *not* sound confident.

'Surely? . . . a chief inspector.' McQuilly seemed surprised at Harris's unvoiced doubts.

'A detective chief inspector,' murmured Gilliant.

'In that case . . .'

'Of course he can do it.' Harris tended to glare. 'Your crowd use detective inspectors for run-of-the-mill murders. What gives you the impression *our* men can't do their job just as . . .'

'I assure you, assistant chief constable . . .'

'I think,' Gilliant pushed himself upright from the desk chair as he said, 'in fact I'm *sure* – we could all do with a meal. We have a choice of quite a few first-class restaurants. Commander, sergeant – you, too, Mr Harris – be my guests. We can continue this discussion as we eat.'

Roper glanced at McQuilly for guidance and, for the moment, McQuilly looked undecided.

'*What* "discussion"?' asked Harris, bluntly.

'A certain amount of background information is necessary,' drawled McQuilly.

As he hoisted himself upright, Harris growled, 'So far, it's *all* been "background information".'

'Confidential background information,' expanded McQuilly.

'We can arrange for a private room,' smiled Gilliant.

'In that case . . . ' McQuilly stood up.

42

Detective Constable Dobson risked a quick glance at the man riding alongside him. Cossitter was quite something. For a few moments, before Hobart had left, he'd cracked; the murder of his daughter had torn aside the teak-hard exterior he'd shown to the world – but only temporarily. Now he was back in charge and as tough and as uncompromising as ever.

As he'd climbed into the front passenger seat he'd brushed aside the automatic offer to help. Instead, he'd rammed the feet of his stiffened legs hard against the slope of the car's floorboard, folded his arms and given the impression that he was there till hell manufactured ice-cream. After ten minutes of driving he still hadn't said a word.

good!

'Comfortable?' asked Dobson, tentatively.

'I don't like motor cars unless *I'm* driving.'

'Oh!'

'And now I'm not able to drive – so I don't like cars.'

'Ah!'

After a few seconds of silence, Cossitter said, 'I have a man who drives me around.'

'I see.'

'He lives in the village. A sort of odd-job man – and he drives me around, when necessary.'

There was about half a mile of silence, then Cossitter added, 'My daughter sometimes drove me around.'

Something should have been said, but the truth was Dobson couldn't think of a suitable reply.

'Like all women,' grumbled Cossitter, 'she was a lousy driver.'

'Oh!'

'You're not so damned hot yourself.'

'I – er . . . ' Dobson swallowed, then ventured, 'What am I doing wrong?'

'There's an engine under that bonnet,' snapped Cossitter.

'Well, yes – but . . . '

'Listen to the infernal thing. It's passing messages. All the time, it's passing messages. *Listen* to it. Feel it with your feet – with your hands – respond to what it's saying.'

'I'm sorry, but . . . '

'Get the right revs.' Cossitter seemed suddenly to become alive. 'You don't need a rev counter. Listen, that's all you

100

need do. Forget the road noise and concentrate upon the engine. There's a time to switch gears. Just one time – the engine's time – not when *you* feel you should. Change when the engine wants to change and you won't race and you won't labour. You can't control those horses under the bonnet. Not *control* the damn things. You can either fight 'em or work with them. That's your choice, man. If you work with them you can drive all day without feeling the strain. If you *fight* 'em you'll be knackered long before they are . . . '

The man's daughter had been murdered within the last few hours, but that seemed to mean nothing to him. He was talking about motor cars. Talking about the finer points of driving. He was talking about something which had almost cost him his life – something which had reduced him to something not too far removed from a helpless cripple – but it was still his passion. It was still the only subject which seemed to stir him.

He stared ahead, unblinking, and reminisced about Formula One racing, its characters and its locations.

' . . . the Monaco. Street racing. Like street fighting is to professional boxing. That's the parallel. Only those with guts need climb behind a wheel. Nobody knows who's going to win the Monaco. Nobody! Nobody's favourite . . . '

The nape hairs of Dobson's scalp tingled as he listened while he drove the car towards Haggthorpe and Apple Tree Farm. Cossitter's fanaticism seemed to border upon the paranormal.

' . . . Lauda. Y'know something? Until he either retires or kills himself Lauda stays king. The others know it. Lauda scares them all to hell. He shouldn't *be* there. Nobody who's taken the beating and the burning he once took should even be alive, much less one of the great Formula One drivers. He's been all the way, and out the other side. Every man in that circus believes in omens. Good luck. Bad luck. They're all a little crazy. And, driving against Lauda isn't too far from driving against a ghost . . . '

It was as if Cossitter couldn't stop talking, now he'd

started. Always motor racing, but forever switching and skittering from person to place, from technique to location.

'. . . it's not what it once was. The Le Mans Twenty-four-hour was *the* race, until they took away the start. The race to the cars. That dash across the track! Christ, you had to be nippy. If some spring-heeled bastard beat you to it, he'd be out and away – with you under his tyres – before you even reached your own machine . . .'

43

'Cossitter,' murmured Reeve. They were driving due west and the setting sun blazed a brilliant sunset on the low, far horizon. The sun-shield wasn't big enough to be effective and Reeve squinted into the glare through half-closed eyes. 'Anthea Cossitter,' he repeated. 'The local post office knew her address. You *didn't*. That's not good bobbying, Parker.'

'Out Pinthead Pike way,' protested Parker. 'It's not even in this *division*.'

'Near enough.'

'For Christ's sake! I'm not expected to—'

'Parochial policing,' sneered Reeve.

'Eh?'

'What do you do, Parker? Draw a chalk line across the bloody road? So far, and no farther? Your authority stretches past the boundaries of your beat, Parker. And your responsibilities run alongside. There isn't a wall – a moat – owt like that.'

'Hey!' Parker glared. 'Since when did *your* arm stretch an inch more than necessary?'

'Since this morning.' Reeve raised a hand to shield his eyes from the dazzle of the sun. 'Since you didn't grab that runaway horse. Since we found the woman with a knife sticking out of her.'

'Suddenly we all become very conscientious,' mocked Parker.

'Suddenly,' corrected Reeve, 'we have too much rank camping on the patch. A lot too much rank.'

'I haven't seen any for a few hours.'

'It'll be back, lad.' Reeve spoke with sad conviction. 'I don't know where it's gone – but it'll be back. That, and more besides. It's bad enough when the buggers are back at DHQ. I don't enjoy 'em swinging on *my* ballocks, twenty-four hours a day. All day and every day, forever and ever, amen.'

'They aren't around *now*,' insisted Parker.

'They'll be back,' predicted Reeve. 'And, when they arrive, they'll want to know what we've done and where we've been. They'll want to know why the hell we haven't solved the bloody case. They'll want to know why we haven't done the impossible.'

'So, if it's impossible . . .'

'Shut up, Parker.' Reeve leaned forward to peer into the sun. 'Just remember, they're going to *find* fault. Whatever we do they're going to dig around until they find *something* to moan about. The trick is to make the clowns *work* finding something. Force 'em to bust a gut justifying their existence. They don't like that. They steer clear of anybody likely to make 'em look lemons.'

Parker figured it was a philosophy well beyond the comprehension of a mere beat-basher. He didn't even *try* to understand. Reeve was a berk. Otherwise he'd know the best way of handling the star and crown merchants. In one ear, out of the other. Play dumb. Let *them* work up a head of steam while you watched.

44

She was one of many, but she was unique. She was dead, and she *looked* dead. They always did. Flensing had seen too many bodies to subscribe to the they-look-as-if-they're-asleep theory. Dead people *looked* dead. Always! There was something missing. The soul, maybe? Flensing found himself hoping it *was* the soul. He wasn't sure; his faith wasn't deep enough for certainty. Nevertheless, and with all his heart, he hoped. Because, if what was missing was the soul, it followed that . . . Again, Flensing *hoped* that it followed.

'I'm sorry.'

The ward sister who'd broken the news to Alva Hoyle was not mouthing empty sympathy.

'You did your best.' Flensing continued to stare down at the dead face.

'No . . . I mean this.' The ward sister glanced around at the giant 'filing cabinet' meant to hold cadavers. 'She should have been waiting in the chapel of rest. You should have let us know you were coming.'

'It makes no difference.' The tone was parched and dry. As if the words were being forced across a desert of arid emotion.

He couldn't quite accept it. Then he remembered – nobody ever *did*. The number of times he'd had the miserable task of breaking the news to some shocked wife or husband. And always the disbelief. The refusal to accept the truth in one single package.

Road accidents were different. If they were there when it happened. If they witnessed it. Then, there was acceptance. But otherwise . . . As if there was some natural law which denied the other the right to die without permission. As if . . .

'Her belongings,' murmured the ward sister.

Flensing looked puzzled.

'Her clothes. Her blouses.'

'Keep them.'

'Her wrist watch.'

'Give it to Alva,' he croaked. 'Alva Hoyle. Tell her – tell her to use it. Not as a memento. Not as a substitute headstone. To *use* it.'

'Shouldn't *you* . . . '

'No. You give it to her. Just, tell her . . . that's all.'

He tried to remember her when she was alive. *Really* alive, and not locked in the iron lung. He couldn't – his mind seemed to have fixed itself on to a memory which *always* included that infernal mechanical contraption via which she'd breathed – and he felt guilt because *that* hadn't been part of her. *That* hadn't died.

'The rings.' The ward sister almost whispered. 'The wedding ring and the engagement ring. Do you want . . .'

'Don't touch them!' The anger at his inability to control his thoughts rode the harsh exclamation. Then, in a less angry tone, 'Just the watch, please. Leave the rings. Everything else – it doesn't matter.'

The ward sister sighed, then repeated, 'I'm sorry,' and, again, meant it.

'I'll . . .' His speech stumbled and, for a moment, he clenched his fists as they hung by his sides. Then, he moved his gaze from the dead face and, in a low, but controlled voice, said, 'I'll make the arrangements. The funeral director. He'll – er – he'll do whatever's necessary.'

Without another word – without a backward glance – he walked from the anteroom of the mortuary. The ward sister slid the drawer back into place on its bearinged runners and, once more, that which had been Helen Flensing became one of many . . . and no longer unique.

45

The sun had dipped below the rooftiles of neighbouring houses, therefore the kitchen was already gloomy. There was light enough to see, but it would have been difficult to read. It was that sort of gloom; a lack of light, but without the warmth of enveloping darkness. It matched their mood to perfection.

The instant coffee in their beakers had grown cold, but had

only been sipped. The plate of cracker biscuits on the kitchen table hadn't been touched. Neither of them wanted to eat. They both yearned to say something. Neither of them could find words appropriate to their feelings.

'Shouldn't you go back on duty?' ventured Alva.

'Hobart's a good man. He'll keep things ticking over.'

'It's a murder enquiry,' Alva reminded him.

'Somebody shoved a knife into a woman I don't even know.' Hoyle teased a cigarette from its packet as he talked. His voice was steady enough, but the only emotion it carried was the hint of sad bitterness. 'We don't know why she was killed. Why she's dead. Could be she deserved it. Most of them *do*. Not many decent people get themselves murdered. There's usually a reason.'

As Hoyle lighted the cigarette, Alva said, 'David, my pet, you have a job to do.'

'The chances are she died quicker – easier – than Helen.' The impression was that Hoyle hadn't even heard his wife's words. He smoked the cigarette as he continued, 'It's a lesson policing teaches you. The bastards always have the easy ride. Being good – being decent – it's a mug's game ...'

'That's not true, and you know it.'

' ... Lie, thieve, twist, connive, there's always some purple-minded prat ready to make excuses for you. Think no ill of the dead ... what the hell he, or she, did when they were alive. Why? *Why*, for Christ's sake? Death doesn't wipe the slate clean. It's how you *lived* that matters ...'

'David ... don't.'

' ... It's how Helen lived. How Ralph lives, how you live, how I live. We're not perfect, but we try. Principles. Discipline. Decency. And, for that we're called "Pigs". We're called "The Filth". The filth of the streets call us that. And crap-arsed do-gooders spend every waking minute of their miserable lives explaining *why* they call us that. They invent "reasons". They twist logic inside out in an attempt to excuse the scum of the earth. They ...'

'David! Stop it!'

He closed his mouth, then, very shakily, raised the cigarette to his lips and drew deeply of tobacco smoke.

In a gentler tone, she said, 'You have a job to do, my pet. You have a murder enquiry to see to.'

He nodded.

'I know how you feel.' She touched his arm. 'I know how *I* feel, so I know how *you* feel. Helen. But we can't alter it, and Ralph must be relying on you. Wherever he is – whatever he's doing – he must be relying on *you* to keep things ticking over till he's back on an even keel.'

Again he nodded.

'Stick it, boy,' she encouraged, softly. 'It's tough. It's one of those damn moments. Those times in life when things look impossible. Okay, you're down – we're *all* down – just don't be *out*. Helen wouldn't want that.'

46

It was quite a restaurant. If the truth be told, Gilliant was playing one-upmanship with the two officers from the Met. He was out to show that all the Egon Ronay eating spots weren't within easy driving distance of Marble Arch. He was out to impress and he was succeeding.

For starters Harris had had Prawn Cocktail. The other three had had Chilled Melon. Then had come the fish course. McQuilly had plumped for Scallops Meunière, Roper had chosen Grilled Lemon Sole with Lemon and Herb Butter and Harris and Gilliant had enjoyed Scampi with Tartare Sauce. Now they were waiting for two helpings of Pork Cutlet with Baked Apple, one Gammon with Pineapple and one Prime Rump Steak. All (as the menu assured them) garnished with the appropriate vegetables.

Harris sipped the classy wine which had accompanied the

two courses and eyed his chief constable with barely concealed cynicism. Big nosh – very expensive nosh – and, for what?

Gilliant was no mug, therefore Gilliant wasn't likely to have swallowed all the ten-cylinder hogwash these two London-based super-sleuths had been feeding them. Hot air about the international dope scene. Vapourings about the IRA. Hooey about some undercover creep. But nothing *substantial*. No real reason for them hot-footing it north.

Other than the helicopter crash, of course. That was hidden somewhere in the swill but, so far, nobody had scooped it out.

And now this – the super blow-out.

Gilliant had been as good as his word. The room was above the main restaurant; a private place used, in the main, for business lunches where deals were made and conversations were meant to be well beyond listening distance of the curious. A couple of waiters saw to their needs and, when not carrying food or wine, or removing used crockery and cutlery, they pointedly left the room and closed the door firmly behind them.

Roper lighted a cheroot. It went with the bandit moustache and Harris's lip curled slightly in a half-sneer.

'A nice place,' observed McQuilly, politely.

'We try to be good hosts,' smiled Gilliant.

'But rarely *this* good,' muttered Harris.

Nobody seemed to hear the remark.

'Commander.' Gilliant leaned forward slightly. 'You came north for a purpose.'

'Of course.'

'Forgive me, but are we to be told that purpose?'

'I was under the impression we'd already *told* you.' The surprise on McQuilly's face looked quite genuine.

'No.'

Harris rumbled, 'So far we've had a guided tour around Rotterdam and a run-down on the cock-ups of the international drug control agencies.'

'Assistant chief constable . . . ' Roper removed the cheroot from his lips as he began to speak.

'Sonny!' The interruption was explosive as Harris allowed his pent-up exasperation to surface. He snapped, 'Let's assume you're here for the ride, shall we? On your home turf you may be something they scare grandchildren with. Up here, you're a sergeant jack – and that's *all* you are. Paddle around at the shallow end and leave the deep water to your betters.'

McQuilly raised remonstrative eyebrows and glanced at Gilliant.

'In a nutshell.' Gilliant calmly backed his second-in-command. 'The Metropolitan Police have strange ways and even stranger departments. Up here, we're much simpler souls.'

'Not *so* simple . . . surely?' drawled McQuilly.

'Let us work on that assumption.' Gilliant matched tone for tone. Then, as the door opened to admit the waiters with the main course, 'Later. Back at my office. For the moment, let's enjoy good cooking, and pretend we're all on the same side.'

47

Hobart drove slowly. Until he was clear of the town he kept the car to within a yard of the kerb and, when the kerb gave way to verges and he reached the open country, he stayed the same distance from the grass. Vehicles overtook him and, on the stretches of road where the twists and turns were plentiful, cars and vans tailed behind him awaiting some reasonable stretch in which to accelerate past. Hobart didn't give a damn. Hobart had worries of his own.

Clarence Hobart knew his own limitations. As a youth – as 'Clarry' – he'd been something of a tearaway. A boozy father, a mother who hadn't had much of a clue about home-making, two sisters and three brothers, and all living cramped in a terrace-type house in the wrong quarter of Bradford hadn't made for gracious living. He'd run with a gang and, as he well knew, some of that gang had ended up surrounded by granite walls. It could so easily have been *him*. More than once, he'd dodged court appearances by the skin of his teeth. Not thieving – thank God not *thieving* – but just about everything short of thieving. Gang fights by the dozen. A few broken bones. More than a few visits to a hospital for stitches to the head and face.

That, of course, before he'd met Fiona.

About a dozen of them tear-arsing along Blackpool's Golden Mile. Yate's Wine Lodge had booted them out and they were whirling and yelling their way towards the Pleasure Beach. Bowling Tide and the resort stiff with Bradfordites. Hooliganism? Sure it had been hooliganism – or, at best, high-spirits bordering upon hooliganism. The pavement crammed with holiday-makers and the traffic bumper-to-bumper, and the whole bunch of them elbowing their way south through a shoulder-to-shoulder crowd.

He'd bumped the girl off the pavement edge and directly into the path of a double-decker. Not deliberately. He hadn't consciously seen her, or even noticed her, and decided to push her out of the way. Not *deliberately*. She'd just been there and he'd been like the rest of his pals and demanded immediate passage.

She hadn't been run over. The bus had been travelling slow enough for the driver to drop anchor and *not* run over her. But it had been a very near thing. Near enough for one of her shoes to be crunched beneath the front, nearside wheel. *That* near!

He hadn't been as drunk as he'd pretended he was. In fact, he hadn't been drunk at all. None of them had. They'd merely been drinking . . . and had play-acted the part out of sheer devilment.

And, when he'd realised what had almost happened, he'd stopped play-acting.

110

There'd been the grandfather and grandmother of rows. His buddies – his mates – had dodged through the traffic and hared off along the promenade but, because he stopped to help the girl to her feet, he'd been hemmed inside a circle of outraged people. People enjoying an annual break and who'd seen what had happened. Then the cops had shown up. A sergeant and a uniformed constable. Then, the accusations and the exaggerations.

That, until Fiona had done something pretty stupid but, at the same time, pretty wonderful.

'Look, sergeant, he's not one of *them*. He's not one of the drunks who've been causing all the trouble. He's with *me*, sergeant. We were walking along when he bumped into me and knocked me off the pavement, but only because *he* was bumped into.'

She'd convinced everybody, too. The crowd, the sergeant, the constable. That look of shock she'd put into her eyes had done the trick . . . and they'd *believed*.

More than thirty minutes later, in the comparative privacy of the South Pier, he'd asked her the reason.

'*Did* you do it purposely?' she'd countered.

'Well – no. Of course not.' And he'd been conscious that he wasn't telling the whole truth.

'In that case . . .'

She'd smiled instead of ending the sentence.

Hobart steered the car into a lay-by and switched off the engine. It was necessary that he clear his mind of memories before he drove farther. That stupid son of his had triggered the mental pictures and, perhaps because and for a split second he'd reverted back to what he'd once been, the pictures were more vivid than they'd been for years. The pictures and the realisation of what he might have become.

Even today he couldn't understand what had happened or *why* it had happened.

Only that there'd been a strange and, to him, unaccustomed tranquillity. That had been the effect she'd had on

111

him from the first day of their meeting. The rebelliousness – the frustrated but pent-up anger – which had been part of his make-up had melted and been replaced by a more gentle, more patient, determination to leave some small mark on the world. To be decent. To do nothing of which either he or Fiona might be ashamed.

Had it been a pick-up? Had *she* deliberately taken advantage of a situation in order to enjoy the company of a strange young man?

Fiona? For God's sake, not *Fiona*!

And yet . . .

Certain it was that, as they parted, she'd said, 'We're going to the Tower this evening. Will you be there?'

'I – I . . .' He'd swallowed. 'Maybe.'

'The ballroom. We usually sit in the balcony. Left-hand side, facing the band.'

And they'd been there. Fiona and her parents. He'd been alone. He'd had that much sense; he'd made some excuse to the other members of the gang and left them to go boozing along the sea-front pubs. He'd spruced himself up a little. He'd even worn a tie – a *tie*, on your holidays at Blackpool, for God's sake!

She'd introduced him to her parents, and the introduction had been preluded by a quick, almost secret, half-smile.

Her father had stood up, shaken hands and very solemnly said, 'I'm very pleased to meet you, young man. Fiona's told us how you grabbed her when she was almost jostled under a bus. We're both very grateful, I'm sure.'

Thereafter, they'd shuffled around the ballroom, hemmed in by what seemed to be a hundred-thousand other 'dancers'. They'd strolled through the gloom of the aquarium. They'd sipped weak tea at a table in the roof garden.

Above all else, they'd talked.

It was another new experience for him. To be with a girl of his own age, without the hindrance of an ever-present aim of 'making' her. Not to have to put on an act. Not to over-state, or make himself sound like Superman. To *communicate* – and to know she understood and, in turn, to understand what *she* was saying and know that *she* wasn't exaggerating.

He'd been with her all day and every day for the rest of that holiday. He'd enjoyed meals with her and her parents. He'd experienced a life style he hadn't known existed.

And, after that . . .

They'd written to each other. He'd visited her at her home. Gradually, but very certainly, they'd fallen in love with each other. And, in fairness, he'd had to explain to her father why he didn't ask Fiona to visit his home.

'Don't think I hate them.' He'd felt the blood flush his features as he'd talked. 'Nobody should hate their parents, and *I* don't. Nor be ashamed of them. I'm not that, either. But there's such a lot of us, and we don't live in a nice house like this, and . . . '

'Clarence.' The father had smiled and touched his arm, comfortingly. 'It doesn't *matter*. We like *you*. Fiona, her mother and me. We all *like* you, lad. I'm only pleased my daughter's got herself such a nice, steady chap.'

Then, the wedding. A nice wedding. The father had seen to that. But no invitations to *his* family – *he'd* seen to that. And, as a result, guilt. He'd denied the guilt at first, but it had been there and, maybe to counter the guilt – maybe to justify the decision not to invite anybody – he'd allowed Fiona far more freedom of choice than the average wife. Anything and everything. He never argued. Over the years she'd had some daft brainwaves, but she'd never taken advantage. She'd always *thought* she was doing the right thing, and that had been enough.

He'd already been in the force – a young beat copper – when they'd married and she'd been as proud as Punch. She'd had the wrong idea, of course. She'd been fed the 'Dixon of Dock Green' doolally. Okay, let her believe it, if it makes her happy – that had been the way he'd played it.

And now, this. He'd belted his own son. For a moment,

back there, he'd reverted to his original matrix and – dammit – for the moment he'd *enjoyed* himself. The knowledge – the certainty – that he could still smash somebody like Morgan into a whimpering wretch.

Hobart smacked the steering wheel gently with the heel of his hands. It hadn't been what he'd wanted to do. He'd gone into the bedroom with the intention of *talking*. Arguing. Making the silly young sod see sense. No more than that.

And, now . . .

48

'Cossitter?' said Reeve.

'Oh, aye.' The local wasn't actually sucking a straw. He wasn't wearing a farmer's smock and leggings. Merely that, in the considered opinion of Police Sergeant Reeve, those things *should* have been there. 'Tha means Andy Cossy?'

'Who?'

'Andy Cossy. Very bossy. See? That's wot we call 'im round 'ere. Andy Cossy – very bossy.'

'Hell's teeth!' breathed Reeve.

'Andrew Cossitter?' Constable Parker tried to steer the conversation towards near-normality.

'Aye.' The local nodded. 'Andy Cossy. Very . . .'

'We can manage without the poetry,' interrupted Reeve. He ventured a somewhat more involved question. 'Do you know him?'

'Who?'

'Cossitter.'

Again the nod. It went with the slightly bulbous eyes and the loose-lipped mouth. 'Everybody knows Andy Cossy.'

'He's not at home,' said Reeve.

'Oh, aye?'

'We've been to his house, but there doesn't seem to be anybody at home.'

'Tha knows where 'e lives, then?'

'Yes, we know where he lives.'

'Wot's tha asking me for, then?'

'Eh?'

'If tha knows where 'e lives.'

'He's not at home.'

'Oh, aye?'

'He isn't *there*.' A hint of desperation tinged the words.

'Oh, aye? Wot's tha expect *me* to do about it?'

'Where might he be?' contributed Parker.

'He might be *anywhere*.' The local obviously counted the question as a particularly stupid one.

'You don't know – is that it?' choked Reeve.

'Wot?'

'You don't know where he might be?'

'How the 'ell should *I* know? He never tells *me* where he's going.'

'Does he tell *anybody*?' Parker tried again.

'Aye.' The usual nod accompanied the answer. Then, 'Billy Carter.'

'Who's Billy Carter?'

'He drives for 'im. Does odd jobs about t' garden.'

Reeve asked, 'Where do we find Billy Carter?'

'He's no'an at 'ome.'

'Oh!'

'Out i' Spain, somewhere. Holidaying.'

'With Cossitter?' It was a little like extracting teeth.

'Nay.' The local obviously counted this a daft question. 'Andy Cossy doesn't go far.'

Thus it progressed, but the progression was slow and painful. The local lived in a world of his own; a world in which the next village was foreign territory. But he knew his village, knew all who lived in his village and knew their movements and their personalities.

He knew Andrew Cossitter's daughter.

'By gum, *she* gets 'er own way when she wants it.'

'A bit of a handful, is she?' teased Reeve.

'*I* wouldn't like to say 'er nay.'

'I'm told she's interested in horses,' fished Reeve.

'Hosses?'

'Rides a bit,' amplified Reeve.

'Oh, aye. They'll do owt, them two. As long as it costs brass, they'll do it.'

'Well off, are they?' suggested Parker.

'They addle more brass than tha does,' the local assured him.

Human nature being what it is both Reeve and Parker were curious to know as much as possible about the Cossitter family. The answers came slowly. Not because the local was unwilling to tell all he knew, but rather because his was a very slow and pedestrian way of life and his speech and thought-process were correspondingly creaky.

Nevertheless, as dusk thickened into darkness, they had an address. The address was Apple Tree Farm, near Hagg-thorpe.

As Reeve turned the ignition key and switched on the lights, Parker said, 'I suppose we should.'

'A friend of the murdered girl,' observed Reeve. 'We'd leave ourselves open to a real going-over if we didn't.'

'If they found out.'

'They'd find out.' Reeve slipped the gear-stick into first and moved the car off. 'A thing like that? They *always* find out.'

'*If* she's the murdered girl.'

'All those "ifs".' Reeve moved the gear-stick into second, then into third. 'Keep everything crossed, Parker. You might make a name for yourself.'

'I don't *want* to make a name for myself.' Parker blew out his cheeks in an exhalation of disgust. He muttered, 'Where the hell *is* everybody?'

49

Flensing was one of the 'everybodies' Parker had in mind. And, for Ralph Flensing, this day would be the one day he remembered when he, himself, died. It *had* to be! The day of his marriage, the day he joined the force, the day Helen had been injured. God only knew these, too, had been days to remember. Days from which he measured other parts of his life.

But, this day . . .

He walked because he daren't yet trust himself to go home. His home – *their* home – had, until this day, represented a hope and a dream. The experts – the specialists – had all expressed a firm conviction. That she'd never walk again. That she'd never be able to *breathe* again without high-class mechanical assistance.

He'd never been completely convinced. He'd never completely *believed*. The medics didn't know everything. Time and again, they'd been proved wrong. A terminal disease . . . but the patient had recovered. Permanent paralysis . . . but the patient had walked.

For years it had been his secret, and a secret he hadn't even shared with his now-dead wife. The house had been geared for *two* people. Tableware and chairs for two . . . plus guests. Two wardrobes, one of which was reserved for dresses, coats, hats and shoes for *her*. The home had been the home of a happily married couple. Complete and ready for her return. Subconsciously he'd made believe that her absence was a very temporary thing. That one day – and soon – she'd resume her place in his life, walk into the house and, without effort or inconvenience, pick up where she'd left off.

Their home. But now it couldn't be and he daren't return to it.

To sit there, *knowing*. No more self-deception. No more

wild hopes. No more – *anything*.

He knew himself too well. He'd fire the place and its contents around his ears and sit there waiting for the blaze to put an end to *his* life.

He might still do just that.

Meanwhile he walked, step at a time, to nowhere. Without purpose and without direction. A pulsating ache behind his eyes – stretching up towards his hairline – prevented concentration enough to know *where* he was walking. Whether he was walking away from something or walking towards something. Just walking. Seeing nothing. Noticing nothing. Aware of nothing.

Treading away each second of this terrible day and wishing that he, too, might die and have done with the heartbreak.

50

Hoyle bathed again. It was something to do. Men who study such things might have argued that it was symbolic. He didn't *need* a bath – he had only recently bathed – but the suds and the soaking had seemed necessary in order to remove something far more terrible than mere dirt.

He dressed slowly and with care. From the skin out, he put on newly cleaned garments. Even the tie, the jacket and the shoes.

When he returned to the living room, Alva said, 'Have a snack before you go back on duty.'

'Coffee, please. That's all.'

'Only coffee?'

'Black coffee. Hot and strong.'

'You could be away for a long time,' she said, gently. 'We both know what a major enquiry can do to meal times.'

'My sweet.' A sad smile touched his lips. 'I feel as if I'm just recovering from the worst hangover of my life. I need something to steady me. To clear my head.'

He followed her into the kitchen and, as she prepared the coffee, he talked and she inserted the occasional remark here and there.

'Since earlier, today. Since I called in for a quick clean-up and a snack. God, it seems an *age*. Thirty minutes – thereabouts – that's what I gave myself. Thirty minutes, then back to the enquiry. Time enough for the test-tube crowd to come up with something. Time enough for the pathologist to be able to give a lead. That was the intention. But since then I seem to have lived through an age. It's hard to realise we're still living through the same *day*.'

'Time is a liar, boy. It always has been.'

'You learn something. You have it all taped, then you learn something. Every day you learn something. Like today. No force can cope with murder *and* a major disaster at the same time. Apart from manpower, they're two totally different situations. Like a bank hold-up and a motorway pile-up. Different. Totally different. A different approach. Different priorities. Both on the same day – within hours of each other – and *any* force gets knocked out of its stride. Then, Helen. Helen dying made things a thousand times worse.'

'Helen didn't die deliberately, boy.'

'Ralph's out of things. It's not *his* fault – it's nobody's fault – I'm not *blaming* anybody – but the one time we really *need* a top man to keep the CID on the rails, he isn't available. Hobart's a good man, but he doesn't carry the weight. He needs back-up from the top and Ralph isn't around to *give* him that back-up. *I* haven't been much good, so far, either. And if Harris gets his claws into things it's anybody's guess.'

'You're on your way. Coffee – then you're in there.'

119

51

Parker's embryo beard itched, his stomach rumbled in protest at the lack of food and, because he hadn't had enough sleep, his eyes felt as if grains of sand had worked their way under the lids. Reeve was a complete nutter. More than that, and more surprising than that, Reeve was turning out to be a regular medal-chaser. Had you asked him – had you asked him a mere twenty-four hours previously – Parker would have described Reeve as something of a pain in the arse, but tolerable. A sergeant, happy to *be* a sergeant and, despite his crackpot ideas, not given to shifting too much furniture. Parker would have claimed to know Reeve down to the last stitch in his socks.

Parker now realised how wrong he'd been.

Reeve was off his bloody rocker! Reeve had fanciful visions of clearing up a murder enquiry; of shoving an arm, chevrons and all, down a drain strictly reserved for high-ranking CID clowns.

'You can't be serious, sergeant.' Parker tried outraged indignation as a long-stop. 'You *can't* be serious.'

'I'm serious,' grunted Reeve.

'For Christ's sake! Where's the skin off *our* nose?'

'Stop bitching, Parker. Keep an eye open for that farm. It should be coming up on the right.'

'We aren't at Haggthorpe yet.'

'This side of Haggthorpe.'

'Y'know, Sergeant Reeve.' Parker peered through the windscreen as he protested. 'We could drop some right ballocks with this little lot.'

'We could,' agreed Reeve.

'In that case, why the hell . . .'

'But, the biggest ballock of all,' interrupted Reeve, 'could be dropped at the next HMI inspection. Give those boys a murder enquiry to go at, and they worry it like a dog worrying a slipper. "What did *you* do, constable?" "What enquiries did *you* make, sergeant?" And if you flannel they've got you. Detected or undetected . . . they don't give a damn. So, when it happens, I want to be able to stand up there and blind the buggers with science.'

'Get a commendation, maybe,' grumbled Parker.

'Parker, I don't give a toss about *your* likes and dislikes. Just keep your eyes skinned for that . . .'

'It's there!' Parker pointed as he interrupted.

'Reeve braked, reversed a few yards and turned right through the gates of Apple Tree Farm.

52

The chief librarian stared at the shell of what had once been the library and art gallery and wondered why on earth he'd returned to gaze at what had once been, at its best, an ugly pile of over-embellished Victoriana. Dammit, there'd never been enough shelves, the cataloguing had been at sixes and sevens most of the time and the morons who controlled the purse-strings wouldn't have recognised a good book had it jumped up and snapped at them.

And yet . . .

Part of Thomas Hardy had died in that inferno. Part of Priestley, part of Dickens, part of Conan Doyle. Part of so many great men and great women. Part of their ideas, part of their imaginations, part of that which had made them unique. It was a ridiculous idea, of course – their ideas, their imaginings and their uniqueness would continue – but that a tiny sliver of what they had created had been destroyed. The librarian knew little or nothing about art, would not have minded too much had he been told he would never hear another note of music as long as he lived and claimed not to understand drama and, therefore, found it vaguely boring.

But books . . . ah, *books*.

Great books could be read and re-read a dozen times and

still be enjoyed. A well-written travel book could take you to any spot on earth far faster and in far greater comfort than any jet-propelled aeroplane. Fine essays flicked ping-pong balls of controversy into the air as easily as fairground shooting galleries. Even the thick and steamy 'modern novels' gave superficial evidence of some degree of research and a desire to enliven the workaday norm of the average man and woman.

The librarian loved books and he viewed what was left of the repository of some thousands of them with a sad expression. Some instinct – some 'pull' – made him stride over the barrier the police had erected and stroll closer.

A man in civilian clothes suddenly barred his way.

'Sorry.' The stranger was polite but adamant.

'I worked here,' explained the librarian. 'I was in charge.'

'Sorry,' repeated the man. 'We're searching the ruins.'

'For what?' The librarian looked surprised. 'I thought all the bodies and the injured had been found.'

'Not bodies,' smiled the man.

'In that case . . .'

'The wreckage of the helicopter.'

'Oh!'

'You understand, of course.'

'I suppose so.' The librarian wasn't completely convinced. 'I suppose there has to *be* a reason.'

'That's what we're here to find out.' The man moved his arms from his sides, as if shooing the librarian away from the burned-out shell. He murmured, 'Now – if you don't mind – nobody's allowed near until we're satisfied.'

The librarian climbed back over the barrier. Reluctantly he left the scene of the disaster. As he walked away he tried to find some logical, reasonable reason for his visit. It had not been morbid curiosity. Nor had it been because he'd had nothing better to do. On the other hand, he concluded, no firm reason and no acceptable logic. Merely that there had been destruction of something he'd been fond of. The close of one section of his life.

And, of course, the burning of so many of his beloved books.

53

The pips stopped, Fiona's voice came over the wire and Hobart pressed the first 10p-piece into the slot.

'Fiona.'

'Clarence. Is that you? Has something happened?' There was sudden concern in her voice.

'No. I just wanted to – ' Hobart moistened his lips. 'Is Morgan downstairs yet?'

'No. I'll go fetch him. If you'll just . . . '

'No!' Hobart took a deep breath then, in a quieter tone, added, 'Not Morgan. I – er – I wanted to have a word with *you*.'

Tough guys! The thought flipped through Hobart's mind. Hard-nosed cops belting ten shades of crap out of the ungodly. Well, here was one who didn't. Here was one who *couldn't* – not yet, anyway.

He'd left the lay-by and stopped at the first telephone kiosk. It had been important. *Very* important. A damn sight more important than a fiddling murder enquiry.

'Clarence!' Fiona's voice broke into his thoughts.

'Ah, yes. I thought . . . ' His mouth dried for a moment.

'Yes?'

'Y'see,' stumbled Hobart. 'When I went up to his room, to speak to him.'

'Yes?'

'I – er – I did something.'

'What? What did you do, dear?'

'Morgan,' muttered Hobart.

'Yes, dear. I know you're talking about Morgan.'

'I'm worried,' confessed Hobart. 'I'm worried that I may have let you down very badly.'

'Let *me* down?'

'He'll – he'll tell you his side of the story.'

'He hasn't said anything yet.'

'No – but he will. When he straightens himself up, and comes downstairs.'

'I'm sorry, I don't quite . . .'

'I was angry,' growled Hobart.

'Of course you were. And with cause.'

'I – I lost my temper – sort of.'

'Yes?'

'I – er – I hit him.'

'Oh!'

'I hit him harder than I *should* have hit him – I think.'

'You mean you injured him? Crippled him?'

'No – not crippled him – but I split his lip.'

'Oh!'

'And – and he might have a couple of loose teeth.'

'Oh!'

'I'm sorry, Fiona.' Hobart's words carried a soft, moaning quality. 'I'm truly sorry.'

'Is that why you've telephoned?'

'Yes. Of course. I've let you down. I've let you down badly. I've never raised my hand to him before, but . . .'

'That might be one reason why he's experimented with drugs,' interrupted Fiona.

'Eh?' Hobart stared at the mouthpiece of the telephone.

'Clarence, dear. You haven't used violence against a defenceless child. He's a grown man. He's your son. He's let you down . . . badly.'

'He's let *you* down.'

'All right, he's let us *both* down. Sometimes a thrashing is called for.'

'You're not . . .' Hobart struggled for the right words. '. . . you're not just *saying* that. Y'know – to make me feel better.'

'A thrashing in the past might have saved this one,' she said simply. 'We've tried kindness. We've tried love. We've . . .'

124

'We still love him. *I* still love him.'

'If he doesn't know that, without being told, he's beyond hope.

'But, tell him,' pleaded Hobart. 'When he comes down, tell him we both love him.'

'I'll tell him,' she promised.

'And that I'm sorry.'

'No, I won't tell him that.' There was a pause, then she said, 'What I *will* tell him is that if he doesn't change his ways there's far more where *that* came from.'

'Fiona!'

'My dear.' Her voice was firm and brooked no argument. 'I stand alongside nobody who opposes you. *Nobody*.'

'But, Fiona, I . . .'

'Morgan must learn that. He must learn that he has a magnificent father, and that I have been blessed with a fine husband. I would hope he has sense to realise these things, without having to have them explained to him. But, if necessary, I'll explain them.'

'I'll – I'll ring off,' muttered Hobart, hoarsely.

'It was very thoughtful of you to telephone, dear.'

'I – y'know – I don't have to tell you, do I?'

'No, dear. You don't have to tell me. And *I* don't have to tell *you*.'

54

Detective Constable Dobson tried to hide his worry and, figuratively speaking, trod water like crazy. His had been a moderately unspectacular police career so far, and he would have liked it to have remained that way. Nevertheless, he was no fool and, even without the evidence of the scorched tinfoil, the still-lighted spirit lamp and the curled slips of thin pasteboard, he knew it wasn't stale tobacco smoke which assaulted his nostrils. This was the stench of dope. Heroin.

'And cocaine.' Cossitter seemed to have read Dobson's thoughts. He glared at the rag-doll figure sprawling on the large sofa, and added, 'That one goes for the white stuff. The pot and the smack are reserved for visitors.'

'Is she . . . ' Dobson didn't know how to end the sentence.

'She's out,' snapped Cossitter. 'She's over the self-pity stage – well past the high-jinks spot – she is *out*.'

'Not dead?' breathed Dobson.

'Not yet.' There wasn't a hint of pity in the words. Nor in the added, 'Give her time, though. It'll come – when she's prayed for it enough.'

'Jesus Christ!'

It was a large room, with large furniture and an unnecessary number of scatter-cushions. There was a great deal of untidiness and far too much light from too many standard lamps and table-lamps all of which added unnecessary illumination to that given by the half-dozen wall-lights.

'All that's left of a party that started last night.' Cossitter's voice was low and heavy with disgust. 'Maybe even yesterday afternoon. Maybe a week ago. These crazy bastards don't know Ash Wednesday from Hallowe'en. They go at it till their spark fails, then they miss a few circuits until they come round, then they either stagger home or start up again.' He pointed to the sprawling woman and spat, 'And *that* is my daughter's best friend. *That* crazy bitch.'

The king-sized ash-trays were all full and overflowing. Cigarette stubs were there but much of it was self-rolled rubbish and, again, Dobson recognised the leavings from cannabis. If, as Cossitter claimed, there had been a party, it had been some party.

'Did you ever *see* such a set-up?' Cossitter turned awkwardly on his artificial legs and surveyed the room. The side-tables heavy with discarded tissues and thrown-away magazines. The chairs with their torn and stained covers. The general impression of rotting and ill-used wealth. 'It's like a high-class whore-house,' he snarled. 'It stinks like a Turkish wrestler's jock-strap. And this is where my daughter died. Great God Almighty! *This* is where she *died*.'

126

It wasn't unlike a fairground carousel. Dobson and Cossitter had left for Apple Tree Farm. Reeve and Parker had missed Dobson and Cossitter and they, too, had driven off towards Apple Tree Farm. Now Hoyle was there and, after asking a few pertinent questions at the local pub, his was the third car to head towards Haggthorpe and Apple Tree Farm. Like a merry-go-round. Like a puppy chasing its own tail.

To say nothing of Hobart . . . but *he* was making for Haggthorpe from another direction. *He* wasn't on the roundabout. With luck, Hobart would catch up with it when it stopped.

And yet . . .

The shambles was no greater than many other murder enquiries. The follow-my-leader cock-up was not new. One day, and assuming it took his fancy, some scribe would unknot the threads and present the episode as a comparatively straightforward manhunt. There would be no heroes, because nobody had done anything heroic. On the other hand, there would be no mention of the lack of leadership which in turn led to a lack of co-ordination which (again, in turn) had both uniformed and CID men rushing around like headless chickens.

The day would be remembered as the day a blazing helicopter fell on to the city of Lessford. By Flensing, David and Alva Hoyle it would be remembered as the day Helen died.

But a woman *had* been murdered at Apple Tree Farm, near Haggthorpe.

As they drew into the farmyard area, Reeve said, 'That's Dobson's car.'

'Who?'

'Dobson. Detective Constable Dobson. What the hell's *he* doing here?'

Parker didn't know Dobson. Parker made it his business to know as few fellow-coppers as possible. Reeve was living proof that to know too many other policemen merely made for hassle. To know his own family was enough for Parker. A wife and four kids, all of whom firmly believed in the existence of a money tree, was enough for any man to handle. Who needed creeps who might have things *he* didn't have and who, having boasted about those possessions within earshot of the family Parker, would trigger off a never-ending argument about tight-fistedness? Who *needed* other people?

They climbed from the car and Reeve waved an arm towards the row of stable doors.

He said, 'Check the nags, Parker. See if the one you saw last night is in there.'

'I can't recognise horses.'

'If they're all white we'll know it's not one of 'em.'

'Look, I don't *like* horses. My daughter likes horses . . . but I don't.'

'I don't particularly like *you*, Parker. But I have to work with you. We all have our own crosses to bear.'

'I don't understand the damn things.'

'It's easy. One end chews your fingers to pulp, the other end kicks your head from your shoulders. Stay in the middle and you'll be comparatively safe.'

'For Christ's sake!'

'Check the horses, Parker. I'll see you in the house.'

Parker looked cross, but three stripes *were* three stripes and Reeve was an officious bastard drunk with power. Parker, therefore, wandered reluctantly towards the stables.

57

'You understand,' smiled McQuilly. 'It was meant to happen out at sea. It was certainly not meant to happen over a built-up area.' He paused and the smile melted. 'Our man inside the IRA *has* to be protected. There was a possibility – even a likelihood – that the passenger in the helicopter might recognise him. It was an unacceptable risk.' Nobody saw fit to comment and the smile returned. A fixed smile. The smile of a man explaining the pros and cons of two evils. 'The drug angle. We *must* know when, and if, the terrorists decide to use illegal drugs to get their way. We're ready for it, but we have to get the information in time. *We have to keep our man there.*'

Gilliant nodded, but Gilliant did not smile.

Roper was watching Harris. A Harris whose normally florid face was white with suppressed fury. Harris worried Roper. Harris was of the 'mad bull' breed of coppers; few in number, these days, but when they went on the rampage what they lacked in personnel they more than made up for in nuisance value. Roper could imagine Harris running wild. Bawling and bellowing his news to the nearest investigative journalist. Harris and his kind suffered a certain lack of perspective. Let's sort today out and bugger tomorrow . . . that was *their* way of life.

The shortsightedness of men like Harris made Roper have nightmares.

'That's it then.' McQuilly stood up and stepped nearer to the desk to shake Gilliant's hand. 'We'll leave you to it. Get back to London and sort that end out.'

Gilliant stood up. He nodded, but said nothing. He

129

ignored the proffered hand and, instead, leaned forward slightly with stiffened arms and half-closed fists resting on the surface of the desk.

He said, 'I'm sure you can find your own way out of the building.'

'Of course.' McQuilly lowered his hand.

'Had you not come, we wouldn't have known,' said Gilliant, flatly.

'It was a risk we couldn't take.' McQuilly allowed the false smile to stay in place. He added, 'On the other hand, you might have *discovered*.'

'It's possible.'

'At least we've eliminated *that* possibility.'

'Goodnight, commander.'

'Goodnight, chief constable. Thank you for your hospitality.'

McQuilly and Roper left the office. Gilliant watched them until the door was closed, then he slowly sank back into his chair.

Harris snarled, 'Of all the . . .'

'Cool down, Mr Harris.' Gilliant snapped the words, then, in a slightly less official tone, 'I know how you feel. I, too. But certain truths have to be faced before we leave this office.'

58

Hoyle drove fast, as if to make up for the time he'd taken to accept the death of Helen Flensing. It was a good car. Not a flash expensive job, but one which Hoyle always kept in top nick. In addition to normal servicing, Hoyle diligently drove it to a nearby garage once a month and allowed one of the city's better mechanics to give it a quick check. Tyre pressure, oil, plugs, carburettor, grease points . . . anything. The result was that it started at the first turn of the ignition key and responded like a dream to every pressure on the accelerator. It was needed. In Hoyle's opinion, it was a basic necessity. A triple-niner – something of extreme urgency – and a man could look a prize prat if his car ground and spluttered and refused to do what it was meant to do. Basic necessity. Basic policing. But a little matter never mentioned on any of the high-flying courses coppers of all ranks were required to attend periodically.

Like now. Distance equated with time, and he'd lost enough of the latter to cut down as much as possible on the former. It was, at least, *something*.

He drove with the window down, with his elbow resting on the ledge, and the rush of cool, late-evening air helped to clear his head.

There was little other traffic on The Tops, therefore he was able to drive much of the time with the headlights on 'beam'. A blanket of light which, at each bend, swept the surface of the ling and bracken. Occasionally the beams reflected the eyes of some creature of the wild: green or red and staring back at this mechanical monster which was invading a territory to which it did not belong.

And, for the first time since he'd stepped from the bath, having been told of Helen's death, Hoyle toyed with questions concerning the murder on The Tops.

Why, for example, the horse? It was either kinky or it was necessary. *Two* horses, in fact . . . Hoyle wasn't going to be argued out of his original opinion that two horses had been involved in whatever had happened.

The murdered woman had been wearing riding gear. The full outfit: riding breeches, waistcoat, cravat, riding-boots . . . the lot. It was, in fact, a very 'horsey' set-up.

He was jumping the gun a little – catching up with lost time – but it seemed a fair assumption that the murder victim *was* Anthea Cossitter. On the face of things, Hobart had already checked that lead and would be waiting for him at Apple Tree Farm. Again, hopefully, Hobart would, by this time,

131

have unearthed a few more leads. He might even have got to within reaching distance of whoever had shoved the knife home.

And that, too, was very odd.

Hoyle didn't like knives. They were too handy. Too easily get-at-able. Any tearaway could stroll into the nearest DIY shop and buy a Stanley knife and, as of that moment, he was as dangerous as a tiger with its claws unsheathed. Sports shops carried a murderous selection of 'camping knives' and get to any seaside town and spring-loaded knives – *flick-knives*, for God's sake! – were there to be bought and sold, quite legally, if the purchasers claimed to be a fisherman.

Far too much sharpened steel was available and Hoyle had had enough police experience to know that a keen edge and a sharp point could be as deadly, at close range, as any bullet. Maybe *more* deadly, if only because the clowns who carried guns often hadn't much of a clue about aiming them.

So, okay, the knife was something not too uncommon.

But to knife somebody on a horse!

And that, of course, was crazy – unless, for example, the creep handling the knife was *also* on a horse. Which, in turn, didn't make too much sense.

Therefore . . .

Hoyle took a hand from the rim of the steering wheel and pinched the root of his nose. He'd had one hell of a day. His concentration was as soggy as wet blotting-paper. The best thing to do was to concentrate on driving, reach Apple Tree Farm, then work things out from there.

59

Parker was surprised to find the stable doors still open. He stepped gingerly into the warm and smelly darkness, flashed his torch around a little and located a light switch.

Four stalls, each with a nag in it. A concrete floor littered with straw and manure and too much clonking of steel-shod hoofs as the animals shifted position to make for the peace of mind of a non-horsey type like Constable Parker.

He hugged the wall and muttered, 'Nice horse. Easy, boy. Easy. Nobody's going to hurt you. Nobody's going to whip you. Nothing like that. All I want to do is *look*.'

Four stalls. Four horses. None of them white, but one of them black, and the black one was saddled up and ready.

Ready? But the word 'ready' suggested a future ride, whereas . . .

'No, mate. You're *still* saddled,' murmured Parker. 'You're the sod who nearly ran me down.'

He stepped carefully to the partition between the stalls and, with equal care, put out a hand to touch the horse's flank. The muscles quivered and the hind hoofs rattled on the concrete as the horse moved at his touch.

'Easy, boy. Easy.' Parker pressed himself against the upright of the partition. 'Nobody's blaming you, boy. It wasn't *your* fault.'

The chomping of a bit in the next stall attracted Parker's attention and, taking a deep breath, he forced himself to make further exploration.

This stall was occupied by a *brown* horse. Brown, bay, chestnut – he'd heard his daughter rabbit on when the goggle-box had shown some horse-jumping event – *she'd* have known, but Parker didn't give much of a damn. 'Brown' was good enough for him, and the brown horse, too, had all the paraphernalia dangling from its back. It, too, was still saddled.

The hair of both horses was matted and without the sheen of recent grooming. In addition to the normal cat's-cradle of reins, stirrups and saddle the black had a length of rope hanging from the harness.

Parker eased himself away from the stalls and stood with his back to the wall of the stable again. He found himself breathing heavier than usual – almost panting – and it was something more than his fear of horses which had brought on the breathlessness.

This was *it*, friend. This was the eye of the hurricane. Horses – and these *were* the horses. Not the droppings. Not some massive hunk of horse-flesh bearing down on him from the darkness. These were the real McCoy. The real thing.

More than that, they were the answer to all the hot-shot activity which had been triggered by the finding of the dead woman's body.

Dammit – and despite not wanting to get involved – *he'd solved a murder*!

The realisation made him feel slightly light-headed. He leaned against the wall of the stable and gulped air for a moment.

The black horse rattled its shod hooves on the concrete floor and began to back out of its stall. Parker suddenly realised the obvious. Neither horse was tethered. Neither *could* be tethered.

He gasped, 'Oh, Christ!' made a dive for the safety of the yard, slammed the stable door closed, turned to hurry to the house and sprawled as his foot caught against the mounting-stone.

As he hauled himself upright he saw the approach of a car's headlights.

60

'I'll not have it,' snarled Harris. 'Great God Almighty, I will *not . . .*'

'You'll have it, Bob.' Gilliant's tone carried both sympathy and understanding. 'It might choke you. It might choke *me*. But it's something we've both got to swallow.'

'Be damned for a tale!'

'Who'll believe you?' Gilliant stood up and walked to the booze cupboard as he spoke. 'Who'll believe either of us? Or *both* of us. I know these people. I've worked with them. There'll be nothing. *Nothing!* They'll have removed every scrap of possible evidence. So who'll *believe*?'

'There has to be *some* way,' stormed Harris.

'No.' Gilliant poured two triple whiskies.

'There's a law. There's a . . .'

'Not with these people.'

'God Almighty, they're not above the law.'

'Oh, yes.' Gilliant handed Harris one of the triple whiskies. 'Above the law. Beyond the law. A law unto themselves.'

'Chief constable,' choked Harris, 'these bastards are responsible for a bloody massacre.'

Gilliant nodded, tasted his whisky and returned to the desk chair.

'Eighteen people. Maybe more. Eighteen ordinary, decent people. And just because some crass sod made a complete cock-up of . . .'

'Bob.' Gilliant moved his free hand in a tiny, tired gesture. 'It's *my* patch, too. But this isn't *policing*. This is war. Undeclared war – but war, nevertheless – between the British Government and the IRA.' He sighed. 'And in every war innocent people die and suffer.'

'I'll not have that.' Harris gulped some of the whisky.

'You'll have it.' Gilliant rolled his glass gently between his palms as he continued. 'An undeclared war. But no less of a war for that. And, as sometimes happens, a tacit understanding between the warring parties. In World War Two, it was gas. In *this* war, it's dope. Not to use illicit drugs as a weapon.'

'That's crap. They've fed us a load of crap in an attempt to . . .'

'No,' Gilliant continued to roll the glass very gently between his hands. 'They don't have to feed us crap, Bob. They didn't even have to *tell* us. It's their idea of being polite. Of short-cutting any trouble, assuming we'd made an

135

educated guess. They have a man somewhere in the IRA council. He feeds them information. He does what he can to keep drugs out of the various battlefields. He's important . . . and, as I understand things, he *might* have been identified.'

'So, they kill . . . indiscriminately?' Contempt and disgust weighed the question with disdain.

'Dammit, Harris, we're not talking about policing. We're talking about *war*.' Gilliant tasted the whisky. His tone carried slightly more authority than previously, but it remained understanding. 'We're talking about a mistake. A mistake in timing. We're talking about the lives – or deaths – of men and women over in Ireland. Of secret courts. Of knee-capping. Of terrorism. Of – of . . . damn it to hell, Harris, you *know* what we're talking about.'

'*I'm* talking about Lessford,' growled Harris.

'All right.' Gilliant took a deep breath. He tasted the whisky, then placed the glass at the far corner of the desk. In a quiet, but grim voice, he said, 'We're on duty, Mr Harris. I'm not arguing. I'm not requesting. I'm your chief constable telling you *exactly* where you stand. I want your firm assurance, before you leave this office, that, as far as *you're* concerned, a helicopter crashed on to the centre of this city. That . . . *and nothing more*. If I don't *get* that assurance you're on indefinite suspension from the moment you close the office door.'

'What the hell!' Harris's eyes blazed. 'You can't *do* that.'

'I can do it,' Gilliant assured him, flatly.

'On what grounds?'

'Harris.' Some of the weariness returned to Gilliant's tone. 'There'll be grounds for your suspension. Believe me . . . there'll be grounds. McQuilly and his friends will take care of that. We're talking about your future, Harris. What's left of your police career. We're even talking about your pension . . . which means we're talking about your family.'

'That's – that's foul. That's *disgusting*!'

136

'It is,' agreed Gilliant, sadly. 'Therefore, *be* disgusted, Mr Harris . . . but make the decision.'

61

Cossitter was rasping, ' . . . this is where she *died*,' as Reeve opened the door and walked into the room.

Cossitter and Dobson turned to the face the newcomer.

Reeve said, 'I'm sorry. The door was open.' He glanced around the room, saw the sprawling woman and the surrounding shambles and added, 'What the devil's been happening here?'

'A party,' said Dobson, with a shrug.

'Drug-taking,' snapped Cossitter. Then, 'Where the devil do *you* come into things, sergeant? What's happened to the CID people? We started with a detective inspector, and now we're down to . . . '

'Who the hell are *you*?' Reeve matched tone for tone.

'Cossitter. Andrew Cossitter.'

'The dead woman's father . . . we think,' added Dobson.

'We're down to a uniformed sergeant.' Cossitter ended what he was going to say.

'It seems to me,' said Reeve, dangerously, 'that, for the father of a murder victim, you're an uncommonly long way from being too upset.'

'What "seems to *you*" isn't all that important.'

'Who's she?' Reeve glanced at the unconscious woman.

'A friend of the victim,' said Dobson.

'*If* it's of any interest, Mary Perkins.'

'It's of interest.' Reeve glared at the small man with the stiff legs. He snapped, 'Cossitter, you may count yourself important enough to merit the personal attention of the Home Secretary, but what you've *got* is me.'

'Who the fornicating hell do you think you're talking to, sergeant?'

137

'I could ask the same damn question.'

They were bawling at each other and, or so it seemed, in a room where a murder had been committed and where the atmosphere was still heavy with illegal dope-taking. Dobson turned his head, first to one then to the other, before taking on the role of peacemaker.

He began, 'Sergeant, I think you should . . .'

'You're out-ranked, lad.' Reeve was at full throttle and in no mood for sweet reasonableness. 'If this half-pint pip-squeak thinks he can throw his weight around with *every* copper, it's about time somebody quietened him down.'

Cossitter roared, 'Of all the officious, jumped-up, self-important prats I've ever come across, you – Sergeant Whoever-you-are – take the blasted cake. You storm into the damned room with more puffed-up arrogance than . . .'

'*That's enough!*' Dobson had to shout as he stepped between Cossitter and Reeve. It was wrong. It was *obscene*. This was a murder enquiry and a uniformed police sergeant and the father of the murder victim looked as if they were on the point of going for each other's throats. He gasped, 'Sergeant – Mr Cossitter – both of you . . . for God's sake, cool it.' Then, addressing Cossitter, 'You, sir. The sergeant has a point. I dunno – respect for the dead is what I mean, I suppose – but you should show *some* feelings. *Some* respect. We're doing our best. We're *all* doing our best. It may not seem much to you but, at a guess, there's a reason – a very good reason – why things aren't being done the way you'd like them done. Have patience . . . that's all.' Then, to Reeve, 'And, sergeant, don't suddenly appear out of the blue and pull rank on *me*. I've held the sticky end of this enquiry all day. Nobody to help. Just me, carrying every can that's coming in this direction. If you think I've missed out on something, tell me. But *don't* suddenly arrive and im-mediately act the high and mighty.'

'I'll tell you what you've missed out on,' said Reeve, coldly. 'You've missed out on asking him how the hell *he* knows she was murdered *here*.'

62

Hoyle had had enough for one day. His emotions had taken a beating and, for the first time in his life, he realised that he, too, suffered the universal ailment of 'growing old'. Bed seemed a thing of the past and also a mere possibility linked with an indefinite future. Using past experience as a yardstick, a thousand-and-one questions had yet to be asked and checked out. The loose-flying ends of this murder enquiry had to be caught, gathered together and made to look as if a whole day *hadn't* been wasted. If possible, Harris had to be convinced that they were already treading on the coat-tails of whoever had shoved a knife into the murdered woman . . . and, whatever else he was, Harris was no mug.

Thus the mental meanderings of Detective Chief Inspector David Hoyle as he turned into the gate of Apple Tree Farm, caught a glimpse of a sprawling figure wearing police uniform and slammed on the brakes.

To have run over a fellow-copper would have placed the cherry atop an already sour Knickerbocker Glory!

'I fell,' explained Parker. He was already upright and dusting himself down by the time Hoyle reached him. 'I fell over those bloody step things.'

'The mounting-stone.'

'Yes, sir.' Then, 'Is that what they are?'

'What's happening here?' asked Hoyle. 'Who's with you?'

Parker answered the questions in reverse order.

'Sergeant Reeve. He's in the house.' Then, almost breathlessly, 'I've detected the murder, sir.'

Detective Chief Inspector Hoyle subscribed to the old school of thought, therefore he did not believe in fairies. He explained his beliefs (and his disbeliefs) to Police Constable Parker.

Parker was indignant.

'It's in there, sir.' Parker pointed towards the stables. 'The horses. Two. One of them the one I saw last night.'

The indignation carried conviction enough to make Hoyle figure he just *might* be wrong. Maybe fairies *did* sit around on mushrooms at the bottom of people's gardens.

As they left the stables and returned to the yard, Hobart's car was braking to a halt.

Hoyle's expression carried a strange mix of mild annoyance and genuine surprise. He joined Hobart and moved his shoulders.

He said, 'Inspector, you're not going to believe this . . .'

63

Gradually – very gradually indeed – Flensing's mind steadied. Slowly – oh, so slowly – he pushed a way through the black curtain of despair and forced himself to accept the fact of his wife's death. It had happened, and he couldn't change things. The tears and the heartache were part of the price demanded for the marriage.

Part of his own life was now blocked out, but part of it still remained. From this day, he was alone. He'd have his friends, he'd have his colleagues . . . but he'd be *alone*.

It would be tough. At times it would tear his guts out. But that, also, was part of the price-tag attached to a marriage which had been near-unique.

And better *him* than *her*!

Had *he* died first – had he been run down by a lorry, or something like that – *her* sufferings would have been multiplied by reason of her own helplessness.

Therefore, better him than her.

And although the conclusion sickened him – although it triggered a wave of guilt stemming from the reluctant conclusion that her death was to be preferred to his own – it was a logic he forced himself to accept.

For the rest of his life he might be mentally crippled. Okay

– maybe . . . if so, so be it. Other people had learned to accept this sort of thing. The heartbreak would remain. The sadness and the loneliness would make the rest of his life like a switchback ride; peaks and troughs; plunges into despair but, with luck, enough work to climb high before the next dip into darkness.

His aimless wandering had brought him back to the centre of the city. To where he could see the skeletal shape of the wrecked library-cum-art-gallery. Now roofless and with eyeless windows through which could be seen the night sky and a sprinkling of stars. Like the heart of most cities, Lessford was quiet at this o'clock. The inner-wheel of pubs, clubs, theatres and eating places would be fairly busy. The outer-wheel of the suburbs might show some amount of activity. But here were only shops and offices, banks and municipal buildings, business premises and daytime cafés. Few people *lived* in these streets and, after dusk, few people had reason to walk the pavements. A scattering of cars, a British Rail worker cycling home from the station, a solitary copper pacing his route past the richest picking the city had to offer.

It was very peaceful.

Flensing lowered himself on to one of the benches provided by the Parks Department. He pushed his hands deep into the pockets of his trousers, leaned back and gazed up and past the glare of the street lighting.

Was there?

Not up there, of course. Inter-planetary science had destroyed the once simple beliefs. Out there was only space and gas and more blazing suns than the mind could encompass.

Nevertheless . . . *was there?*

Because, if there *was*, that's where she'd be.

141

64

The curtains had been drawn back, the windows had been opened and already the place was emptying itself of the throat-catching stench of drug-taking. The cool evening air moved the drapes and a <u>few night-bugs were already spinning</u> and dancing around the ceiling lights, the wall-lights and the table-lamps, all of which had been switched on.

Hoyle had set up the confrontation. He had pushed his rank to the limit and, eventually, silenced the rumbustious Cossitter. He had stationed Reeve at the door and Hobart near the windows. Dobson had his notebook and ballpoint at the ready and he (Hoyle) had claimed an armchair at an angle to, and at one side of, the chair occupied by Cossitter.

The woman was still sprawling on the sofa. She had her mouth open and was snoring gently. Hoyle had raised one of her eyelids, then checked her pulse. The drug-induced stupor was moving into genuine sleep. This time she would awaken to a bad hangover. At some time in the future, and unless she changed her ways, there would be no more hangovers. She would sleep forever.

But that was another problem. For the moment, murder held centre-stage.

Parker stood on the outsized sheepskin hearthrug, with his back to the empty grate. This, his moment of glory, had been thrust upon him and, right now, he was not enjoying the experience.

'It's not the usual Interview Room.' Hoyle started the ball rolling. 'That, however, is not important. It *is*, however, an interview. You, Cossitter, have some plain and fancy questions to answer. You've been cautioned. Detective Constable Dobson has noted the time when you were cautioned. He's also noted the rude remark you made immediately *after* you were cautioned. The law requires that

I now assure you that you can keep your mouth shut from here on . . . assuming you're capable of *not* shooting your lip off at every verse end. It won't be held against you. Nobody will take silence as a tacit admission of guilt. Equally, if you feel the need for a solicitor to be present . . . '

'I don't need a damned solicitor!'

'If you require a solicitor – at any time – you're free to pick up that phone and call one.'

'I don't *need* a solicitor.'

'You now know your rights,' said Hoyle, flatly. He nodded at Parker, and added, 'You're at the wheel now, constable.'

'It's – er . . . ' Parker cleared his throat, then moistened his lips. 'Horses, you see. Horses. And your daughter.' He talked directly at Cossitter. 'Last night – in the early hours of this morning – that black horse almost ran me down. The one in the stable. The one still saddled up. It came at me like a mad thing. Full tilt. It scared the life out of me.

'Then . . . ' He paused and again cleared his throat. But, when he continued, his voice was steadier. 'Sergeant Reeve met me shortly after that, and we drove around a while. Not too far. And we found the body of your daughter, with a knife stuck in her. Full riding gear . . . see? The horse. The riding gear. They went together.'

'Is this necessary?' growled Cossitter. 'All this drivel about horses and the clothes my daughter was wearing? Is it *necessary*?'

'*I* think it's necessary,' countered Hoyle. 'And, at the

'Well – it was . . . ' Again, Parker stumbled a little. 'The chief inspector – Chief Inspector Hoyle – thought that two horses must have been involved. He was right, of course – but I didn't altogether agree at the time. Two horses. And – y'know – horses make their own way home, don't they? I mean, like donkeys on the sand at the seaside. They go so far, then they turn round. They won't shift. They know how far to go, then they turn round. Horses. Donkeys. They all do the same.

for to go, when they turn around. Horses. Donkeys. They'll do the same?

'Horses? Donkeys?' Cossitter's scorn made the two words ugly. 'Why not homing pigeons? Why not *everything*?'

'Why *not* everything?' Hoyle's tone was as uncompromising as Cossitter's. 'Cats, dogs, salmon, eels . . . As you say, *everything*. Given time, they all return to base. The two horses did just that. And their base was *here*. At these stables.'

'You rode one of those horses, sir.' Parker had had enough of this pint-sized prat and it showed in the grimness which entered his tone. 'The black one and the brown one . . .'

'The chestnut.'

'I think *you* rode the brown horse.'

'Is that a fact?'

'They're still saddled up.'

'Are they?'

'They haven't been groomed.'

'Haven't they?'

'And you *do* ride.'

'Do I?'

Parker took a deep breath, then said, 'We've been told you ride, sir. One of your neighbours mentioned that you ride.'

'I ride,' said Cossitter, flatly. 'Has that suddenly become illegal?'

'That brown horse. That's the horse you rode, last night.'

'Did I?'

'I don't know much about riding . . .'

'You don't know much about *anything*.'

' . . . but I have a daughter who bores me to death on the subject. People talk to you – like she talks to me – and some of it rubs off.' He nodded at Cossitter's legs. 'They're artificial – aren't they?'

Cossitter nodded.

'There's a step thing outside.'

144

'A mounting-stone,' murmured Hoyle.

'That gets you on its back,' continued Parker.

Cossitter's eyes narrowed slightly, but he said nothing.

'Those legs of yours – those artificial legs – they don't bend much . . .'

'If you mean the knee,' rasped Cossitter, 'they don't bend at all. I can't be bothered with all the straps and . . .'

'That means a long stirrup.'

'Does it?'

'Cowboys ride long-stirrup.'

'Do they?'

'English people don't.'

'Don't they?'

'Unless, of course, they can't bend their legs at the knee.'

There was a silence.

Parker said, 'The black horse is saddled up normal, short-stirrup. The brown horse . . .'

'The *chestnut*, for God's sake! If you're going to be so smart-arsed, use the correct terminology.'

'The *chestnut*.' Parker gave a single nod. 'The chestnut's saddled up long-stirrup. That's the horse *you* rode. You carried the body of your daughter on the black horse.'

From the door, Reeve murmured, 'That's why you knew she'd been killed *here*.'

'It was *her* horse.' Cossitter's voice had changed. There was near-capitulation in there, somewhere. 'She was dead. It was her horse. What's so strange about that?'

65

Flensing threaded the key into the lock, opened the door and entered his home. His brother and sister-in-law hurried into the hall to greet him, and the concern on their faces etched crease-lines around their mouths and eyes.

The woman said, 'Ralph. Where have you been?'

In a mildly accusing tone, the man said, 'We've been worried sick.'

'I'm sorry.'

They followed him into the living room, and the man said, 'We'd have called the police – if you hadn't *been* a policeman yourself.'

'We didn't want to embarrass you.'

'I'm sorry,' repeated Flensing.

'The woman touched his arm, and said, 'We know how you must feel.'

'No.' Flensing moved his arm away.

'We know how you must feel, Ralph,' she repeated. 'When my sister died . . .'

'No. You *don't* know how I feel.' The smile was quick and tight. 'I don't want platitudes. I don't even want sympathy. What I want I can't have. I have to accept that. Now – please – go home.'

'How d'you mean?' The man stared.

'Go,' repeated Flensing. 'You have your car. It's only forty miles. Fifty, at the most. I have certain . . .' He hesitated for a moment, then said, 'I have certain arrangements to make.'

'You mean the undertaker?' said the woman.

Flensing nodded.

'*We* can . . .'

'Not you. Me.'

'What – what about the funeral?' asked the man.

'*I'll* be there,' said Flensing, sadly.

'Just – y'know . . . just *you*?' The man was finding it difficult to understand this brother of his.

'Mainly me,' said Flensing. 'Not many. It's necessary, but it's not a show-piece.'

'*We'll* be attending, of course.' Indignation touched the woman's remark.

'Why?'

'Because she was – she was . . .'

'You very rarely visited her when she was alive.'

'That was only because . . . '

'It was because the sight of her imprisoned in that damned iron lung made you feel awkward. You could only see *that*. You couldn't see *her*.'

'Hey, Ralph . . . ' began the man.

'Go home,' said Flensing, heavily. 'Thank you for coming, but now go home. You've done your duty. It's enough.'

'You're – you're upset,' stammered the woman.

'Does that surprise you?'

'No – what I mean is – you don't *mean* . . . '

'Leave me to whatever it is I have to bear.' The tone was low and harsh. 'Leave me alone. That's all. For God's sake, *go home*.'

66

And now they *were* in an Interview Room. Number One Interview Room at Lessford DHQ. A purpose-built chamber wherein secrets ceased to be secrets. A room whose very dimensions seemed to have been carefully calculated in order to give the appearance of being confined and yet to have freedom enough for limited movement. Whose furniture – a single deal table and three hard-seated wooden chairs – gave an impression of limited comfort but provided no comfort at all. Whose fittings – wood-blocked floor, single radiator, pebble-paned window – suggested limited attractiveness but gave only vague vexation.

Hoyle had decided upon the transportation of Cossitter to the Interview Room. It was vital that, having *almost* coughed, the man with the artificial legs and the quicksilver temper should be removed from an environment which he apparently knew to be an environment which, while being strange to *him*, was very well known to the police. 'Playing on their own ground' was the colloquialism used.

Hoyle had deployed what few men he had at his disposal.

'Inspector Hobart, you stay here at Apple Tree Farm with Sergeant Reeve. Have a good sniff round for drugs, or anything else which might give some sort of a lead to what happened here last night. And, when Sleeping Beauty there returns to the land of the living, take a statement from her. *She*'ll know what happened. I want a minute-by-minute account, and the name and address of everybody who visited. Everybody!'

Then, to Cossitter, 'You, my friend, are under arrest on suspicion of murder. You've already been cautioned – and that still holds. I won't humiliate you by handcuffing you. You'll run neither far nor fast on *those* legs. Detective Constable Dobson will drive you to the nick in my car. It's a two-door saloon, and you'll ride in the rear seat. Constable Parker and I will be immediately behind you, in Parker's car – just in case you think you can try any Hollywood-style take-over antics.'

And later, while on the way to Lessford and within the privacy of Parker's car, 'Right – bring me up to date, please. It's your case, but *I* need to know. Assume I know nothing. Start with the moment you first saw that horse, last night. I need every detail. Everything we can prove. Every last gut feeling you have – whether we can prove it, or not.'

'Sir,' Parker had protested, 'I'm only a copper. A beat bobby.'

'You're a constable. You took an oath. To that extent, we're both equal.' Hoyle had taken a deep breath, then muttered, 'I *need* you Parker. Things – things that don't concern you – things that have little to do with policing – have kept me away from this enquiry. Forget your rank – forget the difference in our ranks – like it, or lump it, without your help this damn case could end up in the Undetected File.'

It had been an appeal even Parker couldn't refuse. *Him* – Parker – king-pin in a murder enquiry. His wife and kids wouldn't ignore every word he said if he could pull *this* one off. Reeve's wings would be well and truly clipped. Headline stuff. A case he could talk about for the rest of his service.

Not that Parker wanted promotion. Hell, no! The last thing he wanted was to lose this cushy beat. But that was okay. With a murder enquiry to his credit he'd have some say in what happened to him.

Just that . . . it had to help, if he could pull it off.

He said, 'Righto, sir. Starting with the horse galloping towards me. This is what's happened . . .'

Hoyle listened.

But Hoyle, be it understood, was also pulling a very personal ploy. Cossitter was in there, somewhere. Chances were Cossitter was the man they were after. But Cossitter was a very crafty individual. He was no thick-headed tearaway. He had to be conned – tripped up, if possible – then coaxed into making a detailed statement. A statement heavy with lies . . . but of course. Meanwhile, back at Apple Tree Farm, Hobart and Reeve should be turning the place over and, when she came round, the dopey bitch on the sofa would make a statement. An equally detailed statement. And if the details of those two statements didn't tally . . . Bingo! Cossitter had real trouble on his hands.

And now they were in the Number One Interview Room. The official forensic confessional. And Hoyle was setting out the stall via which Cossitter could dig a neat hole and pull the dirt in on to his own face.

67

Meanwhile, Morgan Hobart was having the kinks ironed out of *his* young life.

'He hit me.' He stood in the doorway of the lounge and dabbed his lips with a handkerchief which carried the stain of blood. He seemed on the point of tears. 'He *hit* me,' he repeated.

'Yes, dear.' From the comfort of an armchair Fiona

Hobart touched the remote control and killed a particularly boring television documentary. She turned her head and smiled up at her son.

Morgan Hobart moved into the lounge, still dabbing at his lips.

'Mother, he *hit* me,' he said, for the third time.

'You could,' she said, calmly, 'call it the paternal equivalent to a love bite.'

'Eh?'

'And you know all about those – don't you?'

'Mother, you don't understand.' He flopped into the second armchair. 'When I come home, I don't expect . . . '

'You didn't come home, dear. You were *sent* home.'

'I was unlucky.'

'No, dear. You behaved disgracefully.'

'Some of the others were . . . '

'They, too, behaved disgracefully. If you feel so strongly about it you could write a letter to the university people and name names. Then *they*'d be sent home.'

'Good God! I'm not going to do *that*.' He held the handkerchief part-way to his lips and looked suitably outraged at the suggestion.

'You think it's quite acceptable to behave disgracefully – is that it?' she asked, sweetly.

'No. Of course not.'

'Where, then, is your cause for complaint?'

'Father. He came into my room and . . . '

'Oh, *that*?' The smile was as innocent-looking as a baby's gurgle. 'You're lucky, dear.'

'Lucky?'

'He obviously kept his temper.'

'Kept his temper! Mother, I keep telling you, he . . . '

'Had he lost his temper you'd have needed an ambulance.'

'Look, he's – he's not that sort of a man. He doesn't . . . '

'Ah, but he *is*,' she contradicted, gently. 'I didn't marry a ninny, Morgan dear. I married a *man*. I married somebody

150

capable of looking after me. Physically, if necessary. I married the finest man I could find.'

'Oh!'

'You and I . . . ' She leaned forward in her chair a little and clasped her hands upon her knees. She gave the impression of sharing a confidence which almost amounted to a secret. ' . . . you and I are very lucky. I, because of my husband. You, because of your father. Inside that rather cuddly frame of his there is great strength and great control. Whatever he said to you – whatever he *did* to you – was quite deliberate. He meant it. It wasn't a sudden urge. He felt justified, and *was* justified . . . otherwise he wouldn't have said it and wouldn't have done it.'

'He said . . . ' Morgan Hobart swallowed. ' . . . he said I'd to find a job, or leave home.'

'That, then, is what you must do.'

'He threatened to throw me out of my own home.'

'*His* home. *Our* home, if you wish. Not merely *your* home.'

'But, Mother, there aren't any jobs going. Nobody can find a . . .'

'Oh, come now!' she chided, gently.

'Okay – okay . . . what do you suggest?'

'Join the Police Service,' she said, gently.

'You what!'

'That,' she mused, 'is the advice I gave your father, a long time ago. He followed it, and he's done rather well.'

'I'm not – y'know – "police material". I'm not the sort of man . . . '

'My dear, you're not even *that*, yet.'

'What?'

'A man.' There was sadness in her voice. 'You're not the son we dreamed of, dear. You've been a great disappointment.'

'I thought you were on *my* side,' muttered Morgan.

'That's what I mean.' The eyes had a depth of sadness.

151

'That you *need* your mother "on your side", as you put it – at your age – means you're still a child in a grown-up body.'

'Y'mean . . . ' He moved the handkerchief in a vague and helpless gesture. 'You agree with Father?'

'In everything,' she said, simply.

'Oh!'

'It would be very nice . . . ' Her voice took on a dreamy quality. 'It would be very nice if I'd *two* policemen looking after me.'

68

It was one of the classic interrogation set-ups. Not the 'Mutt and Jeff' gag. Not the 'keep-your-eye-on-me-Buster-because-nobody-else-matters-a-damn' con. This was the 'Poker Game' switch. Four of them, huddled together around a table – the Interview Room table. Cossitter sat at one end of the table; the end farthest away from the door. On his right sat Hoyle. On his left sat Parker. Dobson sat opposite Cossitter, and Dobson had his notebook open on the table top and, in his own brand of shorthand, was recording every word spoken.

'A man with something of a temper,' said Hoyle, gently.

'I've heard it said,' agreed Cossitter, grimly.

'I've *witnessed* it,' said Parker.

'A man with a temper,' repeated Hoyle.

'All right. I have a temper.'

The left-right switch of the head was part of the technique. A question comes from somewhere at the back of your neck, you turn your face to answer. The next question – and the next, *and* the next – comes from behind and, eventually, your mental sense of balance suffers. You aren't *quite* ready for the question, because you're not watching the face of the questioner. You can't *anticipate*.

'You ride,' said Parker. 'You ride horses.'

'Big deal. I ride horses. I need the exercise.'

'You ride long-stirrup,' said Hoyle.

'With these damn legs, what else?'

'You rode the brown horse, last night.'

'It's a *chestnut*. Jesus wept, how many more times do I have to . . .'

'You rode the *chestnut*, last night,' said Hoyle.

'I rode the chestnut,' said Cossitter, wearily. 'I rode it in the afternoon . . .'

'*And* last night,' insisted Parker.

'And last night.'

'Midnight gallops,' observed Hoyle.

'It was necessary.'

'Why was it necessary?'

'For God's sake!'

'Why *was* it necessary?' Hoyle repeated Parker's question.

'I had to get home.'

'Home?'

'*My* home. I had to get home.'

'How did you get from your home to Apple Tree Farm in the first place?'

'That's a stupid question, if ever there was one.'

'Did your daughter drive you there?' asked Parker.

'No.'

Dobson looked up from his notebook long enough to insert, 'I don't think he likes women drivers.'

'Don't you?' asked Hoyle.

'What?'

'Like women drivers?' Parker amplified the question.

'Women *can't* drive.'

'Somebody drove – and it wasn't you.'

'Obviously.'

'It wasn't your usual driver,' said Parker. 'He's on holiday.'

'You've been snooping around.'

'We've been asking questions,' said Hoyle. 'Lots of questions.'

'You got the answers, I hope.'

'Enough,' smiled Hoyle. 'Who drove you to Apple Tree Farm?'

'There are such things as taxi firms.'

'You took a taxi.'

'I've just said so.'

'You *and* your daughter?' insisted Parker.

'We didn't take separate cabs.'

'Why Apple Tree Farm?'

'We were going riding. For God's sake, I thought we'd . . .'

'Why not take a taxi back home?' asked Parker.

'Do you need to be told?' The counter-question came from behind clenched teeth.

'Dope?' asked Hoyle.

Cossitter nodded.

'Murder?' asked Parker.

'Anthea was dead,' said Cossitter, flatly.

'Who killed her?' asked Hoyle.

'I don't know the bastard's name.'

'Where did you get the knife?' asked Parker.

'Where did *I* . . . ' Cossitter took a deep breath. 'Of all the crazy, cockeyed questions . . . '

'Where did you get the knife?' repeated Parker.

'We think *you* killed her,' added Hoyle.

'No. No! – *no!* – NO!'

The last denial was almost a scream. He was toppling and all he needed was one last nudge. Hoyle glanced across the table at Parker and Parker took a deep breath.

He said, 'Cossitter, that damned horse almost ran me down. The black horse. The one you used to carry your daughter's body on. Your daughter's horse. The other one – the one with the long stirrups – the *chestnut* – that was *your* horse. That was the one *you* used. Leading the black? Away from the scene? To some isolated spot where she'd be found? To where mugs like coppers might think she'd been killed? That's it, Cossitter. That is *it*! We don't know *why* you knifed your daughter, but that isn't important. With a hair-trigger temper like you own, you don't really *need* a reason. We know *where* you knifed her. We have the knife. We have the body. We know . . . '

'You know damn-all!' The interruption was hoarse with controlled fury. 'You – you dim-witted, thick-skulled idiot. What the devil do *you* know about such things? You and your size twelves. What the hell do people like you know about *anything*?'

'Tell him,' suggested Hoyle, gently. 'Tell us all. Parker's version is all we have, so far. Trim it around a little, and it could stand you in a Crown Court. It might even push a conviction. Who can tell, with juries?'

'It's wrong,' breathed Cossitter. 'It's all to hell.'

'It's all we have,' insisted Hoyle.

'I . . . ' The steam had all gone in that last outburst. Only heartbreak remained. He whispered, ' . . . I don't want my daughter's name linked with dope.'

'Lots of dope at Apple Tree Farm,' mused Hoyle. 'And that's where she was killed. It all adds up, Cossitter.'

'Not Anthea.'

'That's what *you* say.'

'I *know*. Not my daughter.'

'Okay.' Hoyle turned his hands until the palms were on top. 'Clean the muck from her name. You're about the only one able and willing. All we can do is listen.'

69

Harris sat in his car, parked in the drive of his house and, via the glow from the street lighting, saw the wilted growth where his wife had used weedkiller a few days before. That (he decided) was how *he* felt. Knackered, and ready to drop.

Harris was a very simple man. A very basic man. Not for him the nuances and subtleties of grey. As far as Harris was concerned, everything was black or white, and black was 'them' and white was 'us'. Not for him the hints and innuendoes of double-talk. He called a spade a spade and, when necessary, happily called it a bloody shovel.

And, on this day, he'd been jockeyed into a corner by a duo of smooth-talking creeps from the Met, and only after Gilliant had spelled the situation out for him had he really *understood*.

Some undercover crap in Ireland. Some bog-eyed berk whose identity had to be kept a secret. Some IRA clown being shipped to the Emerald Isle via helicopter . . . somebody who had met the undercover man at some moment in the past, and could blow his cover. A bomb on the helicopter and the pilot and the IRA clown blown to Kingdom Come. The lesser of two evils.

Big deal!

As far as Harris was concerned the London prats and the Irish prats could play puss-in-the-corner with each other till hell became an ice factory. But, when citizens of Lessford – *his* patch – were slaughtered as a result of this under-the-carpet hooliganism, *that* was murder. That was *his* concern.

That was when Harris bounced the throttle past the safety gate and went into overdrive.

That was what *should* happen. But that was what wasn't being *allowed* to happen.

Harris shook his head in silent confusion.

Yards and yards of guff about dope peddling. A conducted tour of the Rotterdam dock area. A jumped-up detective sergeant, tarted up like a punk band's Christmas tree, and with more yap than a politician trying to save a lost deposit. But all it boiled down to was eighteen-plus corpses in the local morgue and a bloody great 'Keep Off' sign erected in the name of pseudo-national security.

Not the Harris way. By God, not the *Harris* way!

Murder was murder . . . was *murder*. The reason for his

156

monthly pay cheque. The final justification for a Police Service.

And if he had *his* way . . .

His angry thoughts skidded to a sudden halt.

My Christ, there *was* a murder. Some woman knifed to death out Beechwood Brook way. Away and gone to hell on The Tops. Nothing fancy, nothing 'international', just a plain and ordinary cold steel job which he'd been glancing through when Gilliant had invited him along to meet McQuilly and his monkey. He'd been on the point of nipping along to ginger things up a little.

So, why put off until tomorrow . . . ?

Harris (being Harris) felt almost contented as he switched on the ignition and reversed the car from the drive. Here was something he *could* get his teeth into. There would be cock-ups – there always were, on every murder enquiry – and some as yet unsuspecting copper would duly have his balls trampled into the mud – and Harris would feel *much* better!

70

They listened and they believed. By the nature of their profession their belief was qualified in that it needed final substantiation before it became absolute, but none of them doubted that the woman would give Hobart enough verification to leave no room for doubt.

The facts fitted. The personalities fitted. But, above all, the manner of the telling left no room for doubt.

The story was not told in any deliberately chronological order. Nor was the telling that of a man playing a part. The heartbreak, the agony and the shattered dreams stitched the story together but were not consciously part of the story. Nevertheless, it was a magnificent story . . . even though, at times, its magnificence was tainted with crass stupidity.

It was a story about Formula One car racing. About a man

(the teller of the story) who, since childhood, had known a single, all-important passion. The passion for speed on wheels. He knew all the great drivers, all the top circuits and all the world-class teams. Where other teenagers had crowded football terraces and roared encouragement at eleven men in coloured shirts, this one had begged lifts and slept rough in order to watch heroes race towards a chequered flag, and sometimes die in their attempt to reach it first.

'That's what most of the spectators went to see.' Cossitter stared at the surface of the table and, beyond the table, into a past he could never shake off. 'It's a blood sport, y'know. And that's what they secretly want. Every man and every woman. Blood! They don't give a damn which make gets to the flag first. Which driver. Which team. Give them a pile-up. *That*'s what they want.'

The teenager was wise enough to know the truth of it, but fanatical enough not to care. To him, at least, the combination of speed and skill was what fascinated him. That, and the men who gambled their own lives in a bid to outdrive each other.

He gate-crashed the practices and wormed his way into the crowds at the pits. It wasn't too difficult. These men, whose arteries seemed filled with engine oil, seemed to understand his feelings. Even to share them. They grew to know him. To recognise this youngster who bummed his way from track to track.

'The Indianapolis Five-Hundred. One of the great races. Two hundred laps – five hundred miles in less than four hours. A lot less than four hours. The first time I saw *that* race . . . '

And at the lesser tracks he was allowed to *touch* one of the cars. Then to sit in the driving seat. Then – at last – to actually *drive* one.

'At Croft. One of the lesser circuits. I did the circuit. Not fast. Not really *fast* . . . '

But a team manager was there and recognised some

158

God-given gift. The natural ability to go for a good 'line'. When to swing wide and when to come in tight on the inside. It was there. He hadn't to be taught.

He was encouraged to try for a faster speed. To 'feel' the car pull against the steering and to know, instinctively, when the tyres were going to loosen their grip on the track and send the car into a high-speed skid. The tricks – both legitimate and dirty . . . he learned them all. How to 'close the gate'. How to force a fellow-driver into a turn too tight to handle. How to toss dice with eternity at three-figure speeds.

The élite of the Formula One crowd opened their ranks and welcomed him. The big money and the high living. The best food, the best hotels . . . the best *everything*. This, in return for speed and more speed. For living on a razor's edge. For knowing sleep will bring nightmares and for accepting those nightmares as part of the job, because to counter them with either too much booze or knock-out tablets might make you just that hint less immediate when tomorrow's reactions were called for.

'Nobody gets money *given*. You earn it both on the track and off the track. You earn it by being shit-scared – day and night. There's damn-all glamour in waking up in the small hours, soaking in sweat and knowing you've been awakened by your own screams . . .'

He'd married. One of the less obvious pit groupies. The daughter of some minor peer of the realm and a bitch who'd rolled between the sheets with drivers from all five continents. But that hadn't been important. To have a home. To have a base to which he could crawl and, hopefully, mend his shattered nerves at the end of a season and before the next season began. That's all he'd wanted, but she'd denied him even that.

'Blasted parties. That's all the stupid cow lived for. She knew every Hooray Henry in the world, and the silly sods figured my house as their everlasting home-from-home. She *collected* the crazy bastards . . .'

And yet, somehow – via some accident she could never

159

explain – she gave him a daughter. Anthea. A daughter who was a little like her mother, but even more like her father. A wildcat . . . but with a core of winning ways.

'I couldn't fault her. She was too much like I'd been. Too much like I still was. Her mother didn't give a damn, and we'd fight. Anthea and me. We fought like crazy – but we never *hated* each other. We never *hated* . . . '

Anthea was away at a Swiss finishing school when the accident happened. The mother was long gone. The seventeen-year-old visited each parent in turn and, although the marriage was still officially valid, its validity was merely the vehicle for slightly more snide in the muck and titillation of the gossip columns.

'She loathed visiting her mother. I know – I'm going to *say* that – but it's true. She'd enough sense in her to recognise crappy values in others. The prats her mother slept with sickened her. Some of the hounds even tried to make Anthea. A sort of mother-and-child screwing job. Damn it, she told me. She held one sod off with a broken bottle. *And* she'd have used it . . . '

Then came the accident. A Formula One being pushed to its limit, a sudden summer downpour and an unexpected side-wind. Nobody could have held it. Nobody! The straw bales merely slewed it and sent it spinning sideways into the crash barrier. The car? Some of the spectators still have parts of that car as a memento of the worst crash they've ever seen. What was left was scrap and, somewhere in that scrap, parts of Cossitter's legs.

'Why in hell they let me live I'll never know. I didn't thank them for it. When I knew what they'd done – what they'd *had* to do – I cursed them in every language I knew. I ended at my arse! No legs. Not even stumps worth calling stumps. I was a wheelchair job for the rest of my life. That's what the sanctimonious creeps told me. From a Formula One to a wheelchair. There wasn't enough left to fit normal, artificial limbs . . . '

Anthea arrived and took over. She knew the men who travelled the circuits. The backroom men. And a man who can design a Formula One racing machine can design anything. Artificial legs are a breeze . . . with, or without, stumps.

'It took some learning.' Cossitter seemed to return from the past as he continued his story. He seemed to become aware that he had a small audience. He rubbed his palms together as he continued, 'No knee-joints, y'see. There isn't enough of *me* for the necessary gear to be strapped into position. It's a little like the old, steel leg-irons you used to see on kids . . . but, this time, no legs inside. Topple sideways slightly, swing at the hip, topple the other way and swing in the opposite direction. It's a knack. It's not easy. At first it's bloody painful. But it comes. And it's a damn sight less humiliating than a wheelchair.'

Cossitter paused, and Hoyle murmured, 'You learned to ride?'

'I did. Anthea, again . . .'

The peg-leg routine had almost driven him crazy but, eventually, he'd mastered it. It had brought back some of his self-confidence. Even some of his previous cockiness.

They – Anthea and he – had come north to live. He'd tired of reading about his wife's fornicatory capers and, without much hassle, he'd divorced her and left it to her various bedfellows to provide the required champagne and caviare. Thereafter, he'd adopted the role of fiery-tempered 'squire' to the village community out on the open moors. They'd accepted it, because they, too, were of a breed not given to diplomatic niceties when anything annoyed them.

Anthea had met her old schoolfriend one day, while shopping in Lessford, and from that meeting had come the horsey connection.

The schoolfriend – Mary Perkins – had been nag-mad and the animals were there for the borrowing at Apple Tree Farm.

'It wasn't difficult for Anthea. She'd learned the rudiments at the finishing school place. The Perkins woman didn't seem to mind, and it made for a change of company from me . . .'

Again, it had been Anthea who had suggested a try at long-stirrup horse riding. At first it had been difficult. Even more difficult than learning to walk. But, once mastered, it had extended Cossitter's freedom beyond his wildest dreams.

That had been three years ago and, since then . . .

'Can we concentrate upon last night?' asked Hoyle, quietly.

'She went riding.'

Parker ventured, 'That much we know. She was wearing the full gear.'

'The black was her own horse. I'd bought her the black. We stabled him at the Perkins' place. But he was *her* horse.'

'And the chestnut?' asked Hoyle.

'Mine, I suppose.'

'You only "suppose"?'

'The quietest mare in the stable. Mine – if only because I always rode her. Only me. Animals . . . ' His mouth moved into a quick, sardonic smile. 'The nicest "people" on earth. She stood at the mounting-block and never flinched while I hauled myself on to her back. She *knew*.'

Hoyle caught the eye of Parker and passed messages.

Parker said, 'Mister Cossitter, sir. The murder? The killing? Would you like to tell us how it happened?'

'Oh . . . *that*?' He seemed almost surprised.

'How you killed her?'

'*I* didn't kill her, you damned fool. I tried to *stop* her from being killed.'

162

71

The murderer took the message with some annoyance. The porter at the Hotel Opal had some slight difficulty in pronouncing the word 'McQuilly', but the murderer knew who he meant.

The same light rain was falling as the murderer left the hotel and returned to the Rue Tronchet. He contemplated the idea of a taxi but thought better of it; the telephone he was required to use in an emergency was only a short walk away and Paris, after dark, was a pleasant enough city in which to stroll. Not like London, not like New York. Mugging was not unknown in any major city but, unlike the capitals of the UK and the USA, the French capital wasn't carpeted with wall-to-wall thugs.

The conversation, when it took place, was a thing of double-talk and enigmatic phrases, and this despite the combination of a direct line and scramblers at both ends. Nevertheless, the murderer knew he was on firm ground. He was a professional to his fingertips and somebody had ignored his advice. He had done his best within the limits imposed. Things had gone wrong – a possibility the powers-that-be had airily dismissed before they'd *gone* wrong. Now they were seeking a whipping boy.

'I could quote certain qualifications,' said the murderer. 'Qualifications which, at the time, I brought to your attention.'

'The final outcome left much to be desired,' complained McQuilly.

'Rather messy,' agreed the murderer. 'It's even reached the French press.'

'I want to see you when you get back.'

'I want to see *you*,' countered the murderer. 'Final payment has yet to be made.'

'You'll get it,' promised McQuilly and rang off.

The murderer smiled his confidence and dropped the receiver on to its rest. He returned to the street and, for a moment, wondered why McQuilly had telephoned. Within twenty yards of the building in which the telephone was housed he realised why. As the knife slid between his ribs he realised why and the realisation angered him because it demonstrated his own lack of foresight.

How, in a capital city, can you pinpoint the whereabouts of one man? Answer – make sure he uses a specific telephone.

And, as he was bundled even farther into the darkened alley to die, the murderer remembered McQuilly's last words.

72

The man cracked. It was as sudden, as unexpected and, in its own way, as creepy as it had been before. Almost in mid-sentence the tears spilled over and ran down his cheeks. The facial muscles twitched as he struggled to keep the tremor from his voice. The hands slowly clenched and unclenched at the end of stiffened arms. He must have known the great upswell of emotion, yet he seemed to ignore it. Seemed even to be unaware of it.

Parker made as if to say something – a murmuring of comfort, perhaps – but Hoyle moved his head in a tiny, negative motion and Parker remained silent. This was what they'd worked for. Gradually, but with an awful certainty, they'd been moving towards this moment. Like a rotten tooth being extracted without anaesthetic, it had to come, regardless of the pain.

' . . . not a full man.' Cossitter's voice was low and harsh, but the words were not gabbled and Dobson was able to record them as they were spoken. 'Not a complete man. Only *half* a man. But she worked to make me whole. Whole. If not in body, in other things.

'It was why we fought. Why we argued. She refused to ease off because I hadn't legs. She taught herself to ignore that part of me that wasn't there. She railed at me, swore at me, played hell with me . . . as if I was what I'd been before. It forced me to do the same back at her, until even *I* forgot. To her I was complete. I wasn't a freak. I didn't even *deserve* sympathy. And that's how we played it. That's how she gave me back my self-respect.'

His tongue licked one corner of his mouth. Not because his lips were dry. Because the tears streaming down his face were dribbling into his mouth, like rain running down the cheeks of a man caught in a downpour.

'That was *us*,' he muttered. 'That was how we showed our love for each other. That was how it was yesterday, when we went riding.

'We went riding,' he repeated. He took a deep breath and, the tears still flowing, continued, 'Anthea saddled up, but she didn't help me aboard the chestnut. She never did. That was one of the things we had going. She sat astride the black and waited. But *I* had to struggle up the steps of that mounting-block. And *I* had to get myself into the saddle. Nobody helped me. She wouldn't have allowed them.

'Anyway – I was saying – we went riding. Not fast. I can manage a short canter but, most of the time, it's just walking. The black likes an occasional gallop at the few spots where there isn't a chance of him breaking a leg in a rabbit-hole. Anthea let him have his head a couple of times . . . as usual. Me? I just let the chestnut amble along at its own speed. The air up there is some of the cleanest in the world and, from on top of a horse, you have a magnificent view . . . '

Cossitter seemed unwilling to leave the memory of that last ride with his daughter. He gave an almost yard-by-yard description and, although they were all three anxious for him to reach the point where he entered the farm house, the three listening officers allowed him to tell his story without interruption.

Then, he said, 'Two hours, three hours – no more than

three hours – and we were back at the stables. We both heard the row coming from the house. We thought a party. Then, we thought some sort of an argument. I was all for stabling the nags, ringing for a taxi – the phone was in the hall – then leaving the idiots to get on with it, but Anthea . . . ' He moved his shoulders in a sad shrug. 'Friends were friends, and that Perkins bitch was her friend. That's what you pay for at flash finishing schools. That, and the right knife and fork to use. "Loyalty" – that's what it's called, but my daughter never needed to be taught *that*. What she needed was to be taught who to be loyal *to*.'

'What was happening in the house?' Hoyle asked the question. It was apparent that Cossitter was still jibbing at telling the last part of his story, but that was the part they wanted to hear.

'Madness. Bloody madness.' Cossitter suddenly seemed to realise that he was weeping. He blinked his eyes, then wiped his face and cheeks with the back and the heel of his right hand. 'I'm sorry,' he muttered. 'I'm sorry. I don't usually . . . y'know.'

'What was happening in the house?' insisted Hoyle.

'A party. Some sort of a party.' Cossitter sniffed, then swallowed. 'I suppose it had *started* as a party. Must have done. Started as a party, then got out of hand. Well out of hand.'

'Drugs?' suggested Parker.

'You saw it. You know how it stank. You've been there. You've . . .'

'We'd like *you* to tell us,' interrupted Hoyle.

'There was a row. An almighty row.' Cossitter had regained some of his arrogance. 'Screaming. Bawling and shouting. I recognised Anthea's voice. She was yelling the place down. She obviously needed help.' He paused to wipe his lips with the back of a hand. 'I went into the room, and there she was. Fighting this crazy bastard with a knife . . .'

Parker asked, 'Where did the knife come from?'

'How the devil do I know?'

'She was fighting a man with a knife,' urged Hoyle.

'Like a wildcat.' Cossitter nodded. 'She'd already clawed his face and she was hanging on like grim death to the hand with the knife. The others were watching. Enjoying it . . .'

Parker asked, 'How many others?'

'Damn it, I didn't stop to count. Half a dozen. Thereabouts. The Perkins cow was there, screaming bargee language at the top of her . . .'

'What did *you* do?' encouraged Hoyle.

'I dragged her out of there. What else?'

Parker asked, 'You fought them?'

'The hell I fought them!' Cossitter glared. 'With no bloody legs, who can fight! I grabbed her by the scruff of the neck and dragged her out into the yard. It was the wrong thing to do.' His voice lowered to a growl of self-disgust as he repeated, 'It was the wrong thing to do. It gave the bastard with the knife the opportunity he was waiting for. She had to loosen her hold and he drove the knife home.'

'You dragged her out,' said Hoyle, quietly. 'Still by the scruff of the neck?'

'How else?' Then, 'I want that bastard tracing. I want him found and charged with murdering my daughter. I want him . . .'

'When you say "by the scruff of the neck",' insisted Parker. 'Do you mean . . .'

'I mean what I say. Backwards. I grabbed her by the coat – by the cravat – and hauled her backwards and out into the yard.'

'Did she struggle?' asked Hoyle.

'Of course she struggled. Dammit, man, it was a madhouse. The noise, and some moronic bastard fighting to stick a knife into her. Wouldn't *you* have struggled?'

Parker asked, 'How long did it take you?'

'Eh?'

'To get her out into the yard? Out of the house?'

'How the hell do *I* . . . ' He quietened, then said, 'Long enough. *Too* long. She'd quietened by then. She was unconscious. She was *dead*.' He paused to take a deep breath, then repeated, 'She was dead.'

'And then?' asked Hoyle.

'Not to have her found there.' Cossitter looked surprised that the question should have needed to be asked. 'Not to have her found there. My daughter – not *there*. Not in *that* blasted company.' A strange agitation gradually took over. His tone took on a quality which wasn't far removed from pleading. He was telling the truth, and nobody doubted that it was the truth if only because it fitted facts which would not have fitted any other explanation. Nevertheless, he made the truth sound like a lie in his over-eagerness to be understood. He stumbled, 'I panicked. Of course I panicked. Anybody would have panicked. You'd have panicked – any of you. She was dead. I *knew* she was dead. I've seen too many stiffs – on the track and off – not to know she was dead. Calling a doctor wouldn't have helped. She was dead. And the knife was still there. It was murder – and at *that* place!

'All right. You're coppers. You're all wise after the event. I shouldn't have done what I did. But I *did* it. I left the knife in. Certainly I left the knife in. She'd been killed. Murdered! I wanted *that* to be known. I didn't want to hide *that*. Just that *where*. I wasn't thinking straight – all right, I wasn't thinking straight. I was in the devil of a corner, so I wasn't thinking straight. But I honestly thought I could shift her body to where it would be found – away from *that* bloody place – and that, as long as the police had the murder weapon, they'd be able to trace the bastard who shoved it in. That's all I wanted. Not to cover things up. Just to make sure the damn tabloids didn't hawk it around that *my* daughter was mixed in with the drug scene. I didn't want that. And they would – they'd have done that, for sure . . . and I didn't *want* that.'

Again his fingers began to clench and unclench. The emotion was there. More emotion than he could handle and yet, because of the type of man he was, he fought to keep it under control. To prove that, even without legs, he was the

168

toughest man – the proudest man – within a moon's march.

'I draped her over the black's saddle.' He started again and the agitation, although not as bad, was still there. 'The black knew her. He was *her* horse. He – y'know . . . he didn't mind. I fastened her, as well as I could, with the stirrups and reins. It was a hell of a job. The knife . . . see? I didn't want to touch the knife. Fingerprints. I wanted to leave the fingerprints there for you to find . . .'

'No fingerprints,' murmured Hoyle.

'It doesn't matter now, does it? *Now* it doesn't matter. That damned Apple Tree Farm has to come into it – so it doesn't *matter*, now.'

Hoyle allowed a sympathetic smile to touch his lips, and Cossitter noticed the change of expression.

'Don't laugh at me, man!' he snarled.

'I'm not . . .'

'Sat astride a bloody horse, at night. Leading another horse, with your daughter's body aboard. Dropping the body off near a main road, in the hope that some passing motorist might spot it, and . . .'

'I was *not* laughing at you, Cossitter,' Hoyle said quietly. Then, with hidden warning beneath the words, 'Police officers lack that twisted sense of humour. We see too many scoundrels. We can tolerate the occasional fool.'

'You think I've been a fool, then?' The question was almost a challenge.

'Haven't you?' Hoyle turned the question back to the questioner and Cossitter grunted.

'You – er . . .' Parker cleared his throat. 'You dropped your daughter off, at the side of the road. What then?'

'I sent the black home to its stable. Then, I rode the chestnut to my own place, then sent *her* home. Then, I tried to drink myself unconscious – but couldn't.'

That, then, was the story. That, then, was the end of it, and Dobson flexed cramped finger muscles as the four of them sat in a pool of silence.

169

In a heavy voice, Cossitter added, 'You're right, of course. I behaved like a fool. I panicked like crazy and did all the wrong things. Even when I reported her as Missing from Home – a damn stupid thing to do. But I wanted to know what was happening. Whether she'd been *found*.'

'Constable Parker, here, found her.'

'Ah!'

'And she hadn't been murdered.' Hoyle made it a soft, throw-away remark, then, before Cossitter could either understand or react added, in a louder voice, 'We'd like a statement, Cossitter. As detailed a statement as possible. Tonight, if you feel up to it. Detective Constable Dobson's notes will form a basis for the statement and Police Constable Parker will be the officer to whom you *make* the statement. As detailed as possible – if you don't mind.'

'Of course.' Cossitter frowned, as if he'd missed something. As if something had slipped past him unnoticed, which, in fact, it had. He cleared the frown and added, 'Of course I'll make a statement. Why the devil shouldn't I?'

'No reason at all.' Hoyle smiled and stood up. 'Meanwhile, I'll check up with Inspector Hobart. See how things are progressing at the Apple Tree Farm end of things.' Then, to Parker, 'Oh, and, constable.'

'Yes, sir.'

'You'd better come with me for a few moments. See what *is* happening, then you can keep Mr Cossitter in the picture. And, while you're at it, fix up tea and biscuits.'

73

'A mild cock-up,' observed McQuilly. 'Unfortunate, but it happens sometimes.'

'Paris?' Roper was carefully fingering his way through numbers contained in a ring-folder as he asked the question.

'Our fairy friend should be with the *real* fairies by this time.'

'Drastic,' murmured Roper.

'Certainly,' McQuilly corrected. 'With Harris making threatening noises up at Lessford . . .'

'Is he?'

McQuilly drawled, 'He's a weak link. He thinks policemen should have consciences. If he ever traced the man who put the explosive device together we'd have problems.'

'The man favoured a timing system.' Roper continued his examination of the numbers as he talked. 'It might have been more reliable.'

'The boat was in position.' McQuilly sounded as if he was tired of repeating the same set of facts. 'The wavelength was agreed. The damn explosion should have taken place over the Irish Sea. Somehow the pilot lost his way. He shouldn't have *been* over Lessford. He was miles to the north. What the hell he was *doing* so far north we'll never know.'

'With a timing system . . . ' began Roper.

'Since Brighton – since the Thatcher bomb – everybody is suddenly hooked on timing systems. Damn it, sergeant, you know the score. You set a timing system, and that is *it*. It works, or it doesn't work. It can blow too early, or it can blow too late. The imponderables get in the way of any degree of real certainty. Whereas, with a radio wave . . . '

'With a radio wave . . . ' Roper pinned one of the numbers with a stiffened index finger. He looked up and grinned, then repeated, 'With a radio wave – with an ultra high frequency radio wave – you don't even need a mid-ocean transmitter.'

McQuilly looked puzzled.

'The index of police radio wavelengths.' Roper glanced at the ring-folder. 'Lessford police car frequency. *Our* frequency – the one we intended to use from the boat . . . '

'No!' McQuilly leaned forward and read the UHF number indicated by Roper's finger. He breathed, 'My God!'

'Wouldn't Assistant Chief Constable Harris do hand-stands,' chuckled Roper. 'Wouldn't it make his day if he knew one of his own squad cars triggered off the bomb.'

74

'I don't believe it,' snarled Harris. 'I do *not* believe it.'

'I'm sorry, sir. I know it was originally reported as a murder, but . . . '

'You had a body. Am I right?' barked Harris.

'Yes, sir. But . . . '

'A body with a knife sticking out of it?'

'Yes, sir. But . . . '

'Out on those bloody moors, somewhere?'

'Yes, sir. But . . . '

'Found by a copper called Parker and a sergeant called Reeve?'

'Yes, sir,' sighed Hoyle.

'Found at some God-forsaken time last night.'

'But not murder, sir.'

'Don't be so damned thick, chief inspector.'

'The knife missed all vital organs.' Hoyle was becoming increasingly annoyed with this pig-headed assistant chief constable. He added, 'And *that*, sir, is a direct quote from the pathologist's report. It is *not* an opinion – mine or anybody else's.'

'Of all the infernal . . . '

'She was dead when the knife went in.' Hoyle increased the volume and shouted Harris down. 'And that, *too*, can be found in the post-mortem findings. She died from strangulation.'

'Hoyle, if you're trying to pass the bloody . . . '

'Damn it man, her father strangled her. *Accidentally*. Trying to drag her away from the man who was *trying* to knife her. The knife went in too late. She was already dead – *and* it missed all the right spots.' Hoyle found time to take a deep breath and let out a sigh. 'All we have is *Attempted* Murder coupled with a coroner's verdict of Accidental

Death. That, and a fistful of drug offences.'

'Drug offences!' Harris seemed to choke on the words.

'Dope,' explained Hoyle. 'The place was like an eastern opium den. The room stank to the high heavens. I've never *seen* such a . . .'

Hoyle was startled to find himself talking to himself. Harris had hurried from the office – apparently in disgust.

75

The dawn did not come up like thunder. Instead, it tiptoed its way into the meteorological records accompanied by a damp mist which added nothing to what few delights it could offer.

Flensing half-noticed it arrive through the uncurtained window of his living room. The realisation came, and went, with no more impact than the flicked memory of a moment before his own world collapsed; of a now unimportant belief that there had been a *first* explosion before the helicopter had blown itself to smithereens.

Police Constable Parker shivered as the early dampness touched his skin and seemed to cling to his embryo beard. He noticed the lightening sky and figured himself hard done by. For a time it had been interesting – even exciting – but, after a few hours of sleep, the price would have to be paid. Statements, reports, summaries of evidence and God alone knew what else, all in triplicate and all assembled into a file inches thick . . . and all by *him*. Appearances at a Coroner's Court, appearances at a Magistrates' Court, appearances at a Crown Court. Bucketfuls of evidence to be given and, for sure, scores of snide questions to be answered from a small army of hungry cross-examiners.

Detective Inspector Hobart and Police Sergeant Reeve were already abed, after taking statements and organising the arrest of various whoopee types who, the evening before, had formed the members of a drug session at Apple Tree Farm.

Andrew Cossitter mourned the death of his daughter in his own self-destructive manner and refused – despite all evidence – to accept the fact that *he* had killed her.

As for Hoyle . . .

'A cock-up,' he admitted sadly as he threaded his legs into pyjama trousers. 'A complete and absolute cock-up, and when Harris gets his second wind, he'll be like a raging bull.'

'It's his job.' Alva Hoyle comforted her worried husband from the warmth of the waiting bed. 'It always *was* the job of the high and mighty to find fault in those over whom they exercise control.'

'In that case he'll have a flag day,' grunted Hoyle.

'You've straightened the tangle.'

'I damn near made it a *bigger* tangle.'

'David, boy . . .' She patted the empty pillow. 'Sleep. That's all you need. Sleep and a clear head. After that, you'll handle Harris and we'll both do what we can to see Ralph over the rough spots.'

Which is what any good police wife might have said . . . but the dawn brought another day, and another day brought a new bundle of problems.

And the problems – both solved and unsolved – were what policing was all about.